A kiss is just

Ariel hesitated. "What happened last night ... between us, I mean ... mustn't happen again. We'll be traveling together...." She took a deep breath. "You know what I mean."

A smile quirked the corner of Matt's mouth. "Yes, I know. And I agree that since this is a business undertaking, we shouldn't mix business with pleasure."

"That's fine, Matt. I just wanted to make sure we understood each other."

"I'm sure we do," he said solemnly.

Maybe if she put a bag over her head and took to wearing tents instead of snug little T-shirts and jeans, he'd be able to keep his hands off her. Maybe.

He remembered how she'd felt in his arms last night, the way her lips parted under his. His body tightened with the memory of it, and almost angrily he moved away.

Dear Reader,

When two people fall in love, the world is suddenly new and exciting, and it's that same excitement we bring to you in Silhouette Intimate Moments. These are stories with scope and grandeur. The characters lead lives we all dream of, and everything they do reflects the wonder of being in love.

Longer and more sensuous than most romances, Silhouette Intimate Moments novels take you away from everyday life and let you share the magic of love. Adventure, glamour, drama, even suspense—these are the passwords that let you into a world where love has a power beyond the ordinary, where the best authors in the field today create stories of love and commitment that will stay with you always.

In coming months look for novels by your favorite authors: Kathleen Creighton, Heather Graham Pozzessere, Nora Roberts and Marilyn Pappano, to name just a few. And whenever you buy books, look for all the Silhouette Intimate Moments, love stories *for* today's woman *by* today's woman.

Leslie J. Wainger
Senior Editor and Editorial Coordinator

Danger in Paradise

BARBARA FAITH

Silhouette Intimate Moments

Published by Silhouette Books New York

America's Publisher of Contemporary Romance

SILHOUETTE BOOKS
300 East 42nd St., New York, N.Y. 10017

ISBN: 0-373-07332-1

First Silhouette Books printing April 1990

Books by Barbara Faith

Silhouette Intimate Moments

The Promise of Summer #16
Wind Whispers #47
Bedouin Bride #63
Awake to Splendor #101
Islands in Turquoise #124
Tomorrow Is Forever #140
Sing Me a Lovesong #146
Desert Song #173
Kiss of the Dragon #193
Asking for Trouble #208
Beyond Forever #244
Flower of the Desert #262
In a Rebel's Arms #277
Capricorn Moon #306
Danger in Paradise #332

Silhouette Special Edition

Return to Summer #335
Say Hello Again #436
Heather on the Hill #533

Silhouette Summer Sizzler

"Fiesta!"

BARBARA FAITH

is very happily married to an ex-matador whom she met when she lived in Mexico. After a honeymoon spent climbing pyramids in the Yucatán, they settled down in California—but they're vagabonds at heart. They travel at every opportunity, but Barbara always finds the time to write.

Chapter 1

The heat from the Santa Ana winds hit Matt McKay full blast, and he smothered an oath. The temperature in Los Angeles had soared to over a hundred degrees, making tempers flare and sending anyone with any sense off to the beach or an air-conditioned movie. Which is where Matt would have been right now if Emory Winston hadn't disappeared with the bank's money.

Most of the time Matt wore a tailored "vice president of the bank"-type suit. But he wasn't in Beverly Hills today as the bank's vice president, he was here as their troubleshooter, a position he took on when a case called for special handling. And the Winston case called for very special handling.

A year and a half ago, against Matt's advice, movie mogul Emory Winston, using the Beverly Hills home as collateral, had borrowed twenty-five million dollars from Continental Trust Investments to make *Winter Love*. There'd been problems from the first day of shooting—

delay after delay, a change of leading men after the picture had already started, union troubles and bickering on the set. Two months ago everything had fallen apart; Winston had disappeared and so had the money the bank had loaned him.

There was only one person who probably knew where Emory Winston was, and that was Winston's stepdaughter, Ariel. She'd been his administrative assistant on the film, so she had to have known what had been going on and where Winston was hiding out.

Matt walked on past the other cars parked along the street, and as he started up the circular driveway he reviewed what he knew about Ariel Winston. A spoiled rich girl, she'd been raised with the best of everything, and that included private schools in Switzerland, expensive cars and designer clothes. She'd dated half the eligible men in Hollywood, and six months ago she'd announced her engagement to Paul Conrad, an actor of dubious reputation.

Matt didn't believe everything he read, but he'd bet his next cold beer that Miss Ariel Winston had been around the track more than once and that she knew exactly where her stepfather and the missing millions were.

A lot of people had gathered on the broad stairs leading to the doorway of the Winston home. Many of them, Matt knew, were simply curious, because today was for looking; the auction wouldn't start until tomorrow. By Friday it would be over, and by then, with any luck, he'd have gotten close enough to the stepdaughter to have gained her confidence and maybe to have learned something.

Parked in the driveway was the blue Mercedes convertible that he knew belonged to her, at least for today.

By the end of the week it would be gone just like everything else.

Well-dressed matrons, businesslike men and women and curiousity seekers pushed their way into the hotel-lobby-sized living room where everything had been tagged. Pretty young women passed out champagne and hors d'oeuvres amid the buzz of conversation and exclamations of awe.

Matt looked from room to room, unable to believe the opulence. There were two grand pianos in the music room and thousands of leather-bound books in the floor-to-ceiling library bookcases. One wood-paneled room held back-lighted cases filled with Mexican and South American artifacts that Winston had collected over the years. The dining room seated over fifty, and the kitchen looked big enough to feed an army.

He stepped outside to the patio, where the water in the swimming pool sparkled blue in the glare of the sun. A tennis court and terraced lawns lay beyond.

Matt, eyes squinting in the sunlight, looked back at the mansion and shook his head. The house in East Los Angeles where he and his three brothers had grown up had had five rooms. In the room he shared with his brothers, there'd been four beds side by side, a dresser and one closet, which worked out okay because none of them had more than one pair of jeans and a couple of shirts at a time, anyway.

He didn't begrudge anybody who could afford to live well, but Emory Winston had taken money that didn't belong to him. It was Matt's job to find Winston and bring him back to face justice and repay the investment company which had invested so heavily in his latest movie venture. The only lead Matt had was the stepdaughter.

When Matt went back inside he headed for the ball-room, where tomorrow's auction would take place. It had been filled with tables on which item after item was displayed, all carefully watched over by both the security people and employees of the auction company. Matt stopped before one of the tables and picked up a bronze Remington. It was a beautiful piece, something he would have traded in his high-rise condo to own. He looked at the tag, whistled and started to move on just as a music box began to play.

He stopped, because the tune, "As Time Goes By," had always been a favorite of his. He'd been in his teens the first time he'd seen *Casablanca*, and for weeks after-ward he'd gone around trying to walk and talk like Bo-gart.

A buxom lady with be-ringed fingers and long red fingernails had lifted the top of a silver music box. Head tilted to one side, she listened to the tune, while Matt waited for her to put it down so he could see the price. If it wasn't too much, he might—

"That's not for sale," a young woman on the other side of the table said.

"It's tagged." The buxom lady frowned. "If it's not for sale, it wouldn't have been tagged."

The young woman came around the table. "I'm sorry," she said, "it shouldn't have been." She put her hand out. The other woman glared, then thrust the mu-sic box at the young woman.

Of medium height and slender, with a strangely waif-like look, the young woman had sun-streaked blond hair that hung to her shoulders and uneven bangs that came just to the top of her brows. There were patches of fa-tigue under her gray eyes, and she'd eaten all of the lip-stick off her full lower lip.

"Well!" The other woman looked her up and down. She pursed her small mouth and said, "Seems to me, Miss High and Mighty, that people who've stolen from other people shouldn't be so particular about what they will or won't sell to pay off their debts."

With that she turned around and tottered off on her four-inch heels.

Ariel Winston's bottom lip quivered. She closed the lid to still the music, and a look of intense pain crossed her face. It was a look that made Matt want to reach out and touch her, to do something, anything, to make the look go away.

And because he couldn't think of anything else to say, he said, in his best Bogart imitation, "Play it again, Sam."

Ariel hesitated.

"If you can stand it, so can I." He smiled at her. "I've seen the movie at least twenty times, but I still can't get his voice right."

The flicker of a smile curved Ariel's lips. "Every time I see it I tell myself I'm not going to cry when Elsa leaves, but I always do." Indicating the music box, she said, "My mother gave this to me on my sixteenth birthday. She and my stepfather bought it in Paris."

"We'll always have Paris," Matt said.

Ariel smiled again, and he felt a jolt all the way down to his toes because he hadn't expected her to be like this, to look like this. The simple white dress she wore gave her the appearance of fragility. Her face, devoid of makeup except for a faint trace of lipstick, made her look younger than the twenty-six he knew her to be.

But that was just a look, Matt told himself. He wasn't going to be fooled by it or by her.

"Is there anything in particular you'd like to see?" she asked, breaking in on his thoughts.

Matt shook his head. "My name's McKay, Miss Winston. I'm with security, here to keep an eye on things." He handed her the ID card that had been arranged for by the Beverly Hills Police Department. It gave his height as six-foot-one, his weight as one-ninety-five. Eyes blue, hair brown. He looked grim-lipped serious in the attached photo.

Ariel handed the card back to him. Holding the music box in one hand she extended her other hand and said, "How do you do."

It was a polite gesture, something he wouldn't have expected from her.

"I've seen your picture in the newspapers," he said.

Ariel winced. "And read the stories?"

"Not all of them."

She straightened her shoulders. "If you'll excuse me, I've got to speak to the people who're handling the auction."

"This must be difficult for you."

She tucked a strand of sun-streaked hair behind one ear. "Yes, it's difficult," she said, and turned away.

Matt watched her move through the throng of people, and his brows drew together in a frown. It must be hard as hell to see everything go, to have the house she'd grown up in taken away, all of the things she loved being pawed over by strangers.

Then his face hardened because he remembered that her crooked stepdaddy was waiting in the wings with what was left of the twenty-five million he'd absconded with. He ought to save his sympathy for the suckers who'd invested their money in the million-dollar swindle.

But there was something about her, something in the rigidity of her shoulders and the way she held her head that touched him. And he cursed Emory Winston for having drawn her into this.

Ariel nodded to the fussy little man in a pinstriped suit. "I'll be upstairs if you need me for anything," she said. "How's it going?"

"Very well indeed." Henry Smythe opened the black notebook he'd been carrying and looked at it. "The art dealers are having a field day. Hotchkins from the Simpson Gallery has his eye on the Miró, and a Miss Emma Pritchard of San Francisco is determined to have the Chagall. Four or five collectors will be bidding against one another for the Mexican and South American artifacts. I should think you'd do quite well with them."

Ariel's hands tightened around the music box. Of all of the objets d'art that belonged to the family, the artifacts were what she hated most to part with. Her mother, when she'd been alive, had been an avid collector. That's how she'd met Emory. They had both gone to an auction much like this one, and they'd bid against each other for a Peruvian Pachacamac pitcher. Emory had outbid Ariel's mother, but that night, to make up for it, he'd taken her to dinner. They were married two months later. "It was the only way I could get my hands on the pitcher," her mother had been fond of saying.

Ariel, whose own father had died when she was a baby, had been five at the time, and Emory had adopted her. She still remembered the day he'd brought her and her mother here. "You're my little girl now," he'd told her. "And this is your home."

Emory was the only father she'd ever known. She didn't believe, would never believe, what everyone said about him. There had to have been a reason why he'd gone away without telling her.

He hadn't gone to the studio the day he had disappeared. "I've got some things to go over here at the house," he'd said. "Tell Irv I'll be in tomorrow and tell him to do whatever he has to to keep that numskull Mancini in line."

Ariel had said she would and refrained from asking why Emory had replaced Ken Cameron with Steve Mancini in the first place, because, in her opinion, Mancini had all the emotion of a dish of cold oatmeal.

The film hadn't been going well from the beginning. There'd been production delays and trouble on the set. When they ran over budget Ariel expressed her concern.

"It'll be all right," Emory had assured her, "even though we've already spent part of the first loan. I'll get the money we need to finish the picture."

She wasn't sure where all of the money had come from. A great deal of it had come from the investment company, of course, but the rest of it, according to Emory, had come from a group of investors from Chicago. Ariel had never been sure who they were, and when she'd questioned Emory, he'd said, "Oh, you know, moneyed men who like the idea of being in the movie industry."

There'd been a harried look about him that Ariel had never seen before, a look that had worried her. On the other two films she'd worked on with him he'd talked things over with her. It had been wonderful to come home at night after the day's shooting to discuss the film's progression and to laugh good-naturedly about the vagaries of its stars.

Emory had done that at the beginning of this film, too, but somewhere along the way he'd stopped. Whenever she'd tried to question him he'd assured her that everything was just fine.

The day that she had gone to the studio without Emory she'd returned home anxious to tell him about the latest problem with Steve Mancini—how Laura Fielding, Mancini's co-star, had pitched a royal fit after the sixteenth flubbed take, which of course had been Mancini's fault.

Ariel had rushed into the house and gone directly to Emory's office. But Emory hadn't been there. Instead, on his desk, there had been a white envelope with her name on it.

Ariel still remembered the feeling she'd had when she saw it, the creeping knowledge that something bad was about to happen. With trembling fingers she'd opened the envelope.

I'm going away. Don't try to find me. When things work out I'll contact you. I repeat, Ariel, for both our sakes, don't try to find me.

And she remembered sitting in the chair behind his desk thinking, Why, Emory? Why have you gone away?

The news that filmmaker Emory Winston had disappeared broke two days later. Newspaper headlines screamed that he had absconded with twenty-five million dollars. Reporters called every hour of the day and night. *Variety* said there'd been trouble on the set of *Winter Love* from the beginning, and the *Hollywood Reporter* quoted Steve Mancini as saying he didn't give a damn if they ever finished the picture.

Creditors, investment officials, studio bigwigs and the police had all descended on Ariel. She'd told them the truth, she didn't know where Emory was. But she didn't show them Emory's note.

The house belonged to the investors now, and in another few days so would the money from the auction. All she would be left with were her own clothes, a few pieces of jewelry that had belonged to her mother and the money from the trust Emory had set up for her years ago, money she wouldn't receive until her thirtieth birthday. She had a modest savings account that would last until she found a job. She didn't think she could do that in Hollywood, not with the scandal surrounding the Winston name. She'd have to go to New York or San Francisco to find work.

But first she had to find Emory.

That night, when the buyers and the gawkers and the auction people had gone, Ariel left her room and started down the broad staircase. It was a relief to have the house quiet once more, but she didn't look forward to spending another night alone. Perhaps she'd... Ariel stopped, her hand on the banister, listening.

"Is someone there?" she asked in a voice that sounded too loud to her ears.

"Security." Matt stepped into the hall from the direction of Emory's office.

"Why are you still here?" Ariel frowned. "I thought everyone had gone."

"Just checking things out, making sure the house is locked up tight." Matt came to the foot of the stairs. "It's an awfully big house, Miss Winston. You really should have someone staying with you." And remembering that he'd read somewhere about her being engaged, he asked, "What about your boyfriend, the actor?"

"Paul? He called off the engagement as soon as the story broke about Emory. Right now he's cruising the Mediterranean with an Italian countess."

"Nice guy."

"One in a million." Her lips quirked in a self-mocking smile. "We took a boat to Catalina once and Paul was seasick all the way. I've been hoping for turbulent seas out of Cannes."

Over Matt's laughter she said, "Emory warned me about him. I should have listened."

"Were you and your stepfather close?"

"Yes, of course. But I've never thought of him as my stepfather."

"Would a real father have left without saying good-bye, without telling you where he was going?" Matt raised an eyebrow. "Or maybe he told you and you're keeping it to yourself." His voice hardened. "Did he tell you, Miss Winston? *Do* you know where he is?"

"No, I don't." Her hand tightened on the banister, and she looked at her watch. "Isn't it time for you to leave, Mr. McKay? I'm sure it's been a long day for you."

He wanted to press forward with more questions. Instead, he backed off and said, "It's been a long day for both of us. There's nothing I'd like better right now than a margarita and a thick, juicy steak." Then, as though it had just occurred to him, he said, "I bet you could use a decent meal yourself, Miss Winston. I know a place that I think you'd like. How about having dinner with me?"

"No, thank you."

"We both have to eat. Why don't we do it together?" A note of concern that wasn't altogether planned crept into Matt's voice. "I bet you haven't had a decent meal in days, have you?"

"No, as a matter of fact I haven't, but—"

"But you don't know me. Is that it?" He smiled reassuringly. "I promise to tell you everything you want to know over the first margarita."

"No, really I—"

"C'mon, Miss Winston. I hate to eat alone, and I bet you do, too. It's cooling off now. A drive along the ocean and a good dinner is just what you need."

The thought of having another lonely meal depressed her. But McKay was a stranger. She really shouldn't . . .

"Look," he said, "I'll wait out by the pool while you change. Okay?"

Ariel, tempted now, hesitated.

"Twenty minutes?" Matt asked.

And knowing she shouldn't, she nodded and said, "Yes, all right. Twenty minutes."

Up in her room, Ariel went to the window and looked down at the pool, watching him. Although well dressed, Matt McKay seemed out of place here in Beverly Hills. He looked like the kind of man who'd be more at home in a rough mountain setting or riding a strong black stallion across an open plain. He'd look superbly masculine in outdoor clothes; tight jeans that molded his narrow hips and long legs, a heavy crewneck sweater that emphasized the broadness of his chest and the width of his shoulders. She'd grown up among movie-star-handsome men, but Matt McKay was something else; he was all man from the top of his unruly brown hair right down to his polished loafers. He—

Matt turned and looked up at the house. He saw her, but he didn't wave or nod, he only watched. And held by the stillness of his body, the seriousness of his expression, Ariel gazed down at him until, with a shake of her head, as though to deny the intensity of his gaze, she turned away.

She came down the stairs thirty minutes later wearing a light blue cotton summer dress. She had pulled her hair back off her face into a ponytail and tied it with a blue ribbon. She looked young and fresh and so innocent that it took every bit of Matt's willpower to remind himself that he'd asked her out to dinner because she was the only lead he had to Emory Winston.

As Matt headed out toward the beach, Ariel leaned back against the leather seat and tried to make herself relax and think of happier days; of long-ago summers and beach parties with burned hot dogs and potato chips, gangly young men with high-wheeled Toyota trucks, and stolen kisses while she and a boy watched the sun set over the Pacific on an evening just like this.

At this time of day the world came alive with radiant color. Because she needed to share the moment, Ariel turned to McKay, but she stopped before she spoke because his face, bronzed now by the sun, looked so serious, so harsh. For a moment she felt an almost physical sense of fear because he looked so uncompromisingly masculine and because she didn't know anything about him.

Matt's gaze met hers and a grin softened his features. As though to reassure her, he said, "I'm single and of reasonably good character. I grew up in East Los Angeles, and I speak Spanish like the Mexican kids I grew up with. I like horses and rainy days and fireplaces, cheeseburgers and french fries, and I want my martinis dry. When I get riled up about our ecology or street gangs or homeless people, I read Sandburg and Frost because they give me back my good feeling about being an American. I wear terry-cloth bathrobes and—"

"You sleep in the nude," Ariel finished for him.

Matt laughed. "You looked a little worried. Like you weren't sure it was a good idea to come out with me." He took a chance and covered her hand with his. "Feel better now?"

Ariel nodded. "Anybody who likes cheeseburgers can't be all bad." She rolled down her window and sniffed the salty air. Only slightly curious, she asked, "Where are we going?"

"To a little place I know between Huntington Beach and Costa Mesa. I think you'll like it."

Thirty minutes later Matt turned off onto a narrow gravel road that led down to the beach. "The restaurant's new," he told Ariel. "Not many people know about it yet, but word's getting around. In another few months it'll be jammed."

The gravel road gave way to a paved entrance, and ahead, on a cliff overlooking the Pacific, Ariel saw the restaurant, and a discreet sign that read Rick's Cafe Américain.

She started to laugh. "I don't believe this," she said.

"The owner's name is Rick, and the piano player's name, at least when he's here, is Sam. I thought maybe you'd get a kick out of the place."

It was a funny, thoughtful thing for him to have done, and because her emotions were so close to the surface, her eyes filled with tears. Embarrassed, she shook her head and said, "This is dumb. I'm not usually a crybaby."

"I didn't think you were." Matt stopped the car. He hesitated, then smoothed the tears away with his fingertips.

Her lips quivered at his touch, and suddenly, like a blow to his solar plexus, Matt knew he wanted to kiss her.

"Hadn't we...don't you think we'd better go in?" she said.

He put his hands back on the steering wheel where they belonged.

When he pulled up in front of the restaurant, an attendant in a red jacket took the car. Once inside, Ariel stopped and, looking around her, said, "I feel like I'm really there, here, in Casablanca, I mean. Any minute now, S.Z. Sackall will lead us to a table. Peter Lorre'll be at the bar with Claude Rains, and Sam will start to play 'As Time Goes By.'"

"I don't know about all the rest, but I'll bet you a gold dirham that we'll hear the song before we leave." Matt took her arm and knew it had been worth the drive just to see her smile. "The owner picked up some of the things from the set of Casablanca, and he had the interiors copied," he told Ariel as a waiter approached and led them to a corner table overlooking the beach.

He ordered two margaritas, and when they came, he touched his glass to Ariel's and said, "Here's looking at you, kid." Then made himself say, "This must be a pretty rough time for you."

Her gray eyes clouded.

"Losing everything. Creditors, newspaper men, the movie studio, cops, everybody breathing down your neck. I can't imagine a man who calls himself your father putting you in a position like this."

"Emory doesn't call himself my father," Ariel said defensively. "He *is* my father."

"Even after what he's done to you?" Matt watched her eyes. "There's been talk...speculation that the police think you know where he is."

"Well I don't." Ariel took a sip of her drink, and he saw that her hand trembled. "Emory is a good man. I don't know what happened or why he went away, but I know he didn't take the money.''

''Didn't take the money!'' Matt's eyebrows shot up. ''He took twenty-five million dollars that he'd borrowed from Continental Trust when he ran.''

Ariel put her glass down so hard that some of the drink sloshed out of it. ''He didn't steal that money.''

''Then why did he run away?''

''I don't know.'' She dabbed at the spot on the table-cloth where she'd spilled her drink. ''But he isn't a thief, and he *will* come back.''

''For your sake, I hope so,'' he said quietly.

They ate their dinner almost in silence. He was sorry he'd upset her, because she only picked at her food. But dammit all, he wasn't going to let himself be fooled by her angelic look or her Little Miss Innocent act.

After they'd ordered dessert, he signaled to the piano player.

The black man wheeled the piano to their table. ''Evening, Mr. McKay,'' he said. ''Something special you'd like to hear?''

Matt nodded. Looking at Ariel, he said, ''If she can stand it, so can I.''

''Holy schmolly.'' Sam groaned, then with a sigh he began to sing.

''You must remember this . . .''

The words that had been sung so many times before seemed different this time. Ariel looked across the candlelit table at Matt, and the anger she'd felt only a little while ago faded. The singer's voice drifted over her like intoxicating smoke. She closed her eyes, and it seemed to her she could see the illusion that had been Casablanca and live again the sweet sad story of a love that could never be.

The last words of the song faded away. The man they called Sam wheeled the piano to another part of the room. And Matt McKay, because he couldn't help himself, reached across the table and covered Ariel's hand with his. "You're tired," he said. "I'd better take you home."

"Yes." Ariel smiled at him. "It's been a wonderful evening, Mr. McKay. Thank you."

"Matt," he said. "My name is Matt."

They spoke little on the ride back to Beverly Hills. Matt shoved a Randy Travis tape into the cassette player and turned it down low. Ariel leaned back against the seat and closed her eyes. When her head nodded Matt put his arm around her shoulder to pull her closer. She stiffened, but when he said, "Why don't you have a snooze?" she relaxed against him and in a few moments her breathing evened and she slept.

Wisps of her pale scented hair blew tantalizingly across his face. Her body felt comfortably warm against his, and when she sighed and turned closer he felt the softness of her breast press against his chest. Unbidden, his body tightened and a heavy throb of desire ran through him. He tried to fight it by telling himself she was the spoiled, rich daughter of a dishonest man, a playgirl who'd probably had dozens of affairs. It was his job to con her into trusting him. They were only together tonight because he was sure she could lead him to Emory. She—

A shudder ran through her body, and she whimpered in her sleep. Involuntarily Matt's arm tightened around her. "It's all right," he murmured. "It's all right, Ariel."

But it wasn't all right, of course.

She didn't awaken until he pulled into her circular driveway. She opened her eyes then, and it took a moment for her to remember where she was. Without moving away, she murmured, "I guess I fell asleep."

"I guess you did."

She looked up at him, her eyes still heavy with sleep, her lips slightly parted.

He wanted to kiss her, wanted to feel the tremble of her mouth against his, wanted to touch the breasts that had driven him nearly crazy for the last twenty miles.

But he didn't. Instead, he glanced toward the big house and wondered if she was afraid to be alone in it night after night, and what it might be like for her to wander through the silent rooms.

He made himself get out of the car, and when he went around to her door he didn't touch her or help her out. He didn't dare.

At the front door he asked, "Would you like me to come in with you?"

"No, thank you." She offered him her hand as she had earlier in the day. "I had a lovely time tonight, Matt. For a little while I almost forgot . . ."

She caught her bottom lip between her teeth, and it was all Matt could do to keep from grabbing her. He still had hold of her hand. All he had to do . . .

Ariel stepped away from him. "Goodnight, Matt," she said, and before he could answer she went in and closed the door.

She went directly upstairs, and when she turned out the light in her bedroom she lifted the lid of the silver music box. As she listened once more to the tinkling music she thought about Matt McKay and smiled because his imitation of Bogart was just about the worst she'd ever heard.

As she drifted to sleep, Matt's voice merged with Bogart's, while in the background the last few notes of the music box slowly faded.

Chapter 2

Every sharp clap of the auctioneer's gavel struck like a physical pain, as one by one all the special things Ariel had grown up with passed into the hands of strangers.

When the bidding started on the Chagall, Ariel clenched her hands to her sides and dug her nails into her palms to keep from crying. Her grandfather had bought the painting in Paris during the twenties, and it had always been Ariel's favorite. As a child she had loved its vivid colors and the fanciful, dreamlike quality. She had pretended that, like the birds fluttering about the painted window, she too could somehow fly through it into a magical land of make-believe.

But there wasn't any magical land, and the Chagall, like all of her childhood dreams, was being taken from her.

Finally, because she could stand it no longer, Ariel retreated to the one room in the house where she could, for a little while yet, relive some of those childhood dreams.

She still remembered the first time she'd seen the play-room. Emory had taken her hand, and with her mother a step behind them, he'd led Ariel inside. She'd stood on the threshold, eyes wide with disbelief as her gaze swept over the dolls and the toys, the clowns and the stuffed animals. A two-storied dollhouse, filled with intricately designed furniture and exquisitely made little people, had been set up in one corner. A baby buggy held a curly-haired doll with long lashes. A small table and four chairs had been placed under the window, and the table had been set with child-sized china plates. A carved rocking horse with golden reins waited in the middle of the room.

"I guess you're too old for a rocking horse." Emory had watched her as she'd shyly begun to walk around the room. "But I couldn't resist it."

"I love him," she'd said. "He looks like a prince." She'd smiled up at Emory. "That's his name. He's my Prince."

She ran her hand down the carved head as she had that day long ago and tried not to look at the tag stuck to the once-proud nose.

The other things, the dolls and stuffed animals that the auction company didn't want, she'd box today and send to a children's home in Tijuana. She reached for a red-nosed clown in a pink-and-green polka-dot suit. With the corners of his mouth turned up and his pink hat askew, he looked rakish and debonair.

"You're just what I need to cheer me up," Ariel said and set him aside. With a sigh she took one of the boxes she'd stacked near the door and began to pack away the memories of her childhood.

An hour later she'd filled three boxes and started on a fourth. Totally absorbed in the work she didn't hear Matt until he said, "How about some lunch?"

"Lunch?"

He stepped into the room and waggled a white bag under Ariel's nose. "Cheeseburgers, french fries and chocolate shakes." He grinned at her. "You said yourself that anybody who liked cheeseburgers couldn't be all bad, so let's eat."

Before she could say anything he crossed to the small table. "I don't think we can manage the chairs, but the table ought to do." He sat down cross-legged on the floor and, looking up at her, asked, "You haven't eaten yet, have you?"

"No, but..." Ariel took a deep breath. The burgers smelled good. She brushed her hands against her jeans and sat down across from Matt. "You've got to stop feeding me," she said.

"Why?" Matt spread napkins on the tabletop and placed a burger and a bag of french fries in front of her. "I hope you like 'em with onions." He raised a questioning eyebrow. "You don't have a heavy date later on, do you?"

Ariel shook her head. She hadn't had a date, except for last night, since the scandal had hit the papers.

"I haven't heard from any of my friends for a month or so," she said. "A few of them called when the story first broke. They wanted to know all the details, like why Paul had broken our engagement and what was going to happen to Emory when the police found him. But later, when I called some of them to see if we could have lunch or maybe go to a movie, they made excuses." She looked away. "I got the message."

"Nice people." Matt wanted to take her hand. He wanted to tell her that she didn't need fair-weather friends who wouldn't stand by her when she needed them, or a fiancé who left the country as soon as he'd known she was in trouble.

She wasn't at all what he'd expected her to be. Certainly she didn't look like his preconceived idea of her. She'd pulled her hair back, but a few tendrils had come loose and hung wisp-soft around her face. There was a streak of dirt on the red-and-white-checked shirt and a smudge on her cheek. She looked earthy and disheveled and altogether desirable as she bit into the burger and licked a dab of mustard off her lip.

Matt glanced around the room and tried to picture her sitting on the floor in front of the dollhouse or riding the rocking horse. In his mind's eye he saw the child she had been, dressed in a pinafore, clutching the golden reins of the painted horse as she rode into an imaginary land of childhood dreams. He wondered if she'd had playmates or if she'd played here all alone.

"You didn't have any brothers or sisters, did you?" he asked. And when Ariel shook her head he said, "I have three brothers, two older and one younger. We fought a lot when we were kids, but we had a lot of fun, too." He looked around the room. "Were you ever lonely here?"

"Yes." Ariel reached for a french fry. "Once in a while the children of Emory's and mother's friends came over to play. But most of the time I was alone."

"You didn't mind?"

"Yes, I minded, but like a lot of children who don't have brothers and sisters I created a world of my own. I had an imaginary friend named Myrtle and a cat, a real one, named George. I'd dress him up in doll clothes and try to make him sit in a chair while Myrtle and I sipped our tea."

She took a drink of her shake and a rim of foamy chocolate covered her upper lip before she blotted it away with a paper napkin. Matt wondered what she would have done if he'd leaned over the toy table and licked it away.

To get his mind off that he picked up a french fry and said, "Tell me about your stepfather."

"What do you want to know?"

Where he is, Matt almost said. Instead, stalling while he gathered his thoughts, he took a bite of his cheeseburger. "I don't know." He shrugged. "I'm curious, that's all. All I know about him is what I've read in the papers. I saw the last two pictures he produced, and thought they were good. I guess I'm trying to reconcile your 'good father' image of him with what he did. He took a lot of money with him when he disappeared, Ariel." Matt leaned across the table, his eyes intent on hers. "The police are going to keep hounding you until they find him. There's even talk about a grand jury investigation that'll name you as co-conspirator."

Ariel's face went white.

"So I'm wondering just what kind of man he is to let somebody he professed to love take the fall for him."

"He . . . he wouldn't do that."

"He already has."

"Emory cares about me. If he went away there had to be a reason."

"A multi-million-dollar reason." Matt hardened his voice. "Your stepdaddy's run out on you, sweetheart. Left you all alone to face the music while he's off doing the mambo in Rio."

"Stop it!"

But he couldn't stop now. He had to press hard, try to scare her into telling him what she knew. "Why should you take the rap for what he's done?" he challenged. "If you know where he is, tell the police. It'd be better for

Emory in the long run, and a hell of a lot better for you
if you tell the truth. Why should you—"

"Get out!" Ariel scrambled to her feet. "You don't
know anything about Emory. He didn't . . . he couldn't
have . . ." Her face twisted in anguish, and she hugged her
stomach as though she were in pain.

Matt took a step toward her.

"Go away," she managed to say.

"I want to help you." His face was as white as hers
now.

She turned her back on him, still holding herself,
bending into her grief. "Get out of here," she whispered.

He went out and closed the door, clutching the knob
so tightly his knuckles turned white. "Damn!" he whispered.

The day passed and darkness came. Ariel didn't turn
on a light but sat there in the darkness of the playroom
surrounded by the ghosts of her childhood. At last, when
all of the cars had left the driveway and the house had
become quiet, she went down to the big white kitchen and
fixed an omelet and a piece of toast and carried them on
a tray into the dining room.

Ariel sat in her place at the end of the long table. She
looked down the length of it, and it seemed to her that
she could see and hear the way it had been so many times
before: the ivory damask tablecloth set with the Lim-
oges china, the crystal glasses filled with fine Spanish
wine. She pretended to see again the actresses in their
thousand-dollar gowns, and the actors, not all of them
handsome, but each with that special something that
made him a star. And Emory in his white dinner jacket

at the head of the table, smiling at her over his glass of
wine.

What wonderful times they had had, what a glorious
dream it seemed now.

Finally Ariel carried the half-eaten omelet back to the
kitchen, and when she had washed the dish and the glass
she went out to the lighted patio and stood for a little
while looking out at the pool and the tennis court beyond.

Back inside she made a final tour of the house she had
grown up in. She went from room to room, looking and
touching, for one last time, all of the things that had been
a part of her life.

But that life had ended. In a few more days she would
leave and nothing would ever be the same again.

Matt didn't see Ariel the next day. But the following
morning, the last day of the auction, he caught a glimpse
of her standing in the back of the room. She wore a simple yellow dress, and her face, devoid of makeup, was
very pale. By noon the auction had ended and movers
began taking things away.

He'd thought about her a lot since that lunchtime
they'd spent together in the playroom. He hadn't liked
himself much that day, and though he told himself he'd
only been doing his job, he couldn't forget the tears that
had flooded Ariel's gray eyes or the way she had held
herself against the pain that racked her.

He damned Emory Winston for what he'd done to
Ariel, and himself for making her cry. Whatever part she
had in this, it couldn't have been easy on her, watching
everything she'd grown up with being sold out from
under her. She'd looked a lot unhappier yesterday when
the people came in to pack up the Mexican artifacts than

she'd looked today when they drove the blue Mercedes away.

What would she do now? Matt wondered. Would she bide her time, wait until the scandal cooled down before she made her move? Or would she hop the next plane out of L.A.? Whatever she did, wherever she went, he'd be just a step behind. She was his one lead to Emory Winston; he wasn't going to let her out of his sight.

That night, after everyone had gone and everything had been taken out, Matt sat in his car watching the house. Once he reached in the glove compartment of the car, trying to find a pack of cigarettes, before he remembered he'd quit smoking. Fidgety, he fumbled in the dark for a cassette, shoved it in, then swore because it was the same Randy Travis tape he'd played the night he and Ariel had driven back from the beach. He thought of how it had been that night with the breeze coming in off the ocean, the warmth of her close to him, the scent of her, the softness of her breast pressing against him.

He clicked off the tape and wondered what she was doing now, all alone in the big empty house. What if she fell or got sick or needed something? The phone had been disconnected today. What if somebody broke in? She wouldn't be able to call for help.

"Dammit," Matt muttered and slammed his fist against the steering wheel. Then, because he couldn't help himself, because he told himself it was part of his job to keep track of her, he got out of the car and headed for the house.

When there wasn't any answer to his knock he tried the front door. It wasn't locked. He called, "Ariel?" and waited. She didn't answer, so he went into the entrance hall. From there he looked into the empty living room. The overhead light was on, but she wasn't there. He went back into the front hall, and then he heard it, the faint tinkling sound of the music box. He paused a moment, listening, and went to the foot of the stairs.

She sat huddled there, halfway up, head on her knees, clutching the music box.

He said her name, "Ariel?" and when she lifted her head he started up the stairs.

"Go away," she whispered. She put her head down again, and he knew she was crying.

He stood on the step below her, then quickly, without conscious thought, dropped down beside her and gathered her into his arms. For a moment, her body stiffened and she tried to move away. But Matt held her, one hand behind her head, the other around her back, and brought her up against his shoulder.

He had never seen anyone weep this way before, had never heard this kind of bottom-deep grief. He didn't try to speak because there was nothing to say. He only held her and stroked her back until at last the sobs subsided into hiccuping gasps and she shuddered against him.

His arms tightened around her, and he held her for a long time without speaking. And when she had quieted, he stood and took her into his arms. She sighed and turned her face into his shoulder, too exhausted by weeping to protest.

He carried her the rest of the way up the stairs and down the hall to the room next to the playroom, the room he thought was probably her bedroom. But when Matt opened the door, he saw that it was empty. The bed had been taken away along with everything else in the room. There were two suitcases by the door, nothing else.

"You can't stay here," Matt said as he set her on her feet.

Ariel knuckled the tears away. "I was going to call a cab and go to a hotel, but I forgot the phone wasn't connected."

He picked up the suitcases and started out of the room. When Ariel hesitated, he said, "I'll take you to a hotel."

"I'd...I'd appreciate that." Her hands tightened around the music box. She looked around the room one last time, then followed Matt down the stairs and out of the house without a backward look.

He helped her into his car, then put the two suitcases in the trunk. When he came around to his side and got in, her head was back against the leather seat and her eyes were closed. By the time he pulled out of the driveway she was asleep.

He knew she was exhausted, and the idea of leaving her at a hotel bothered him. She shouldn't be alone tonight. Besides, what if she split? He tapped the steering wheel with his fingertips, and after a moment's hesitation headed toward his condo.

Ariel was still sleeping twenty minutes later when Matt pulled into the parking lot of the condo complex where he lived.

"Ariel?" He touched her shoulder. "Ariel?"

Her eyelids fluttered open.

"Wake up. We're here."

He went around to help her out, and when he did she stood for a moment, trying to get her bearings, shivering a little in the cool night air. He got her two suitcases out of the trunk, then taking her arm led her toward the building.

"Is this a hotel?"

"No, Ariel. This is where I live."

"But I...I can't stay here."

"Yes, you can." Matt tightened his arm around her waist and led her into the elevator. "You shouldn't be alone tonight. I'd feel a lot better if you were tucked safely into my guest room."

She wanted to argue with him, wanted to say, I don't know you, I'm not even sure I like you. But she was so tired it was all she could do to put one foot in front of the other. If she could rest for a little while, just for tonight, she'd be able to think, to decide what she was going to do.

His condo was on the top floor. He switched on a light when they went in. The walls of the apartment were a cool ivory, and the furniture was comfortably masculine. She followed Matt, and when they were in the bedroom she sat on the edge of the bed. He put her suitcases side by side on a bench and said, "Is it all right if I open them? I thought I'd take something out for you to sleep in."

"S'all right," she said sleepily and leaned back against the headboard.

He smiled when he saw the red-nosed clown tucked into one side of the first suitcase he opened. A blue nightgown and matching robe were near the top. When he took them out, he saw a framed photograph. He glanced at Ariel. Her eyes were closed so he picked the photograph up and looked at it. There was a young woman in it who looked like Ariel, a younger Emory Winston and a ten- or eleven-year-old Ariel. The three of them posed in a jungle-type setting. Behind them was an overhang of brush and trees and in the distance a rise of mountains. The young woman had some kind of a pot in her hands.

He turned to Ariel and, seeing that she was awake, asked, "Is this your mother?"

Ariel nodded.

"She was a beautiful woman. You look a lot like her." Then casually he asked, "Where was this taken?"

"In Mex—" She hesitated, and a flush colored her cheeks. "In...uh...in Peru, I think."

He knew she was lying. "What were you doing there? Vacationing?"

"No, we were on a dig."

"A dig?"

"Mother and Emory loved looking for artifacts. A couple of times they signed up to work on archaeological digs, and one summer, the summer the picture was taken, they took me along. It was like digging for buried treasure, and I loved it."

"Looks like pretty rugged country."

Ariel nodded. "We were hours from civilization. We slept in tents, and everybody cooked over an open fire. It was just about the best time I ever had."

Her eyes filled with tears, and because Matt was afraid she was going to start crying again he put the photograph down. He wanted to tell her that things would look better in the morning, but he couldn't because he didn't think they would. "You'd better get out of your clothes and try to get some rest," he said instead. "Are you hungry? Would you like something to eat?"

"No, thank you." She swung her legs off the bed and picked up the gown and robe.

"Call me if you need anything."

"I will." She took a deep breath as though to steady herself. "You're being awfully nice to me, Matt. I don't know what I'd have done tonight if you hadn't..." She let the words trail off, then straightening her shoulders went quickly into the bathroom.

Matt went out into the kitchen. He made a cup of hot chocolate for Ariel, and when he heard her come out of the bathroom he went to the partially open bedroom door and said, "May I come in?"

Ariel, who'd been sitting on the edge of the bed, slipped quickly under the sheet before she said, "Yes, of course." Her face was scrubbed and her hair shone like pale gold in the lamplight. Her shoulders looked cool and white against the blue spaghetti straps of her nightgown; her breasts soft and sweetly rounded beneath the clingy fabric.

Matt cleared his throat and said, "I thought you might like a cup of hot chocolate." He sat beside her on the edge of the bed.

She looked at him and he wanted to say, Don't look at me like that because when you do, I almost forget what my job is. He handed her the cup. She took a sip and said, "This is delicious."

"It'll help you sleep."

"I don't think I need any help." She lay back against the pillows, and he saw how drawn her face was, how tired she looked. When she raised the cup to her lips again, her hand trembled. "Why are you being so nice to me, Matt?" she asked.

"You need a friend," he said uncomfortably.

"Yes, I do. But..." Ariel hesitated. "I don't think you approve of me. I'm not sure why. Is it the way I live... lived? Do you object to that much affluence? Because if you do, it isn't there anymore. Or is it because of Emory? Because you believe everything you've heard or read about him and that it's rubbed off on me?"

She was hitting too close for comfort. "You're wrong about my not liking you," Matt said. "I do. You're a beautiful young woman, and I wanted to help. There didn't seem to be anybody else—"

"You're right about that. There isn't anybody else."

"What are you going to do now?"

"I don't know. I'll find a job. Not here, of course, not with all the scandal. Maybe in New York." She pleated one corner of the sheet. "But first I've got to find Emory."

"I thought you said you didn't know where he was."

"I don't."

"Then how...?"

"I'm not sure." She picked up the photograph that she'd placed on the nightstand when she came out of the bathroom. "I just know that I have to find him." She ran her fingers across the glass. "We had such a wonderful time that summer. My mother was so happy. She..." Tears clouded Ariel's eyes. She put the photo down and covered her face.

"Hey, don't. Don't do that." Matt put his arms around her.

"S-sorry." The tears wouldn't stop coming. "I miss her," she whispered. "Maybe none of this would have happened if she were here. She and Emory were so perfect together. Now she's gone and Emory's gone and I'm alone and that...that scares me."

"Sure it does," he murmured. "Take it easy, Ariel. Things will work out." He put his hand on the back of her head to smooth her hair. It felt like silk against his fingers, and so did the arms that crept up around his neck. She raised her face to look at him, and when she did her mouth was close, so close to his.

"Ariel?" he whispered. And before she could move away he claimed her lips. She trembled in his arms, and that made him feel—God, it made him feel primitive, the strong male who could take what he wanted. And he wanted this woman. Wanted to strip the blue gown off her fragile body so that he could bury his face against her breasts, drink in her scent and her taste, mold her to his body. Possess her.

Her lips parted under his, and he took that full ripe lip between his teeth to kiss and suckle as he'd wanted to from the first time he'd seen her. And when she moaned against his mouth, his body tightened hard with passion.

Without releasing her, Matt eased her further down in the bed. Half lying over her, holding her, he found her breasts. She whispered a protest, but he was past hearing as he fondled their softness beneath the silk fabric of her gown. He touched the nipples and breathed a sigh of pleasure against her lips when they hardened to his touch.

Her hands crept up around his shoulders, and he knew that he could take her now. He could strip the gown away. He could... He felt the dampness of the tears she'd shed earlier against his throat and knew how vulnerable she was.

He hesitated and a shudder ran through his body. He sat up. "Sorry," he murmured. "Sorry."

Ariel lay back on the pillow. Her eyes were misty gray, her lips swollen from his kisses. Her breasts rose and fell with each breath.

"I shouldn't have done that," Matt said. "I brought you here as a friend. I shouldn't have taken advantage...." He got to his feet, and in a voice made hoarse with all that he was feeling said, "I'll be in the next room if you want anything."

At the door he turned and looked back at her, his hand on the doorknob, holding on to it as though it were a lifeline.

"Good night, Matt," she whispered.

"Good night, Ariel." He made himself turn away from her.

She lay very still, looking at the closed door, afraid that Matt would open it again. Afraid that he wouldn't. She didn't know what had made him stop. She didn't know what she would have done if he hadn't. Her body still trembled from his touch, and the arms that had held him felt empty now. She hardly knew Matt McKay, but she had responded to him as she'd never responded to a man before. She'd known him for only a few days, yet he'd set her afire and made her long to be closer to him.

It's because you're lonely, she told herself. The last few weeks, particularly this week, have been terrible. You were reaching out for comfort. He was here and kind and things got a little out of hand. That's all. That's all it was.

But as tired as she felt, a long time passed before Ariel slept that night.

Chapter 3

For weeks Ariel had awakened thinking about Emory, but when she awoke this morning her first thought had been of Matt McKay. She lay without opening her eyes and relived again the moment when he had kissed her.

A reluctant smile curved the corners of her mouth because she knew it hadn't been easy for Matt to turn and walk away. But he had; like an old-fashioned gentleman, he hadn't taken advantage of her vulnerability.

She sensed a strength in him she hadn't seen in other men. He'd be a good man to have on your side in time of trouble, and if what he'd said about a grand jury investigation naming her as co-conspirator was true, she was in trouble.

With a sigh Ariel opened her eyes and boosted herself up on the pillows. She picked up the framed photograph on the nightstand and studied it for a long time, not sadly as she had last night, but thoughtfully. She'd lied to Matt about its having been taken in Peru; it had been taken in southern Mexico, somewhere between Oaxaca and Tehuan... She wrinkled her forehead, trying to remember the name of the town further down south from Oaxaca. As near as she remembered the site of the dig had been halfway between those two cities and down toward the coast. She couldn't remember exactly where because it had been a long time ago and the site of the dig wasn't as well known as either Mitla or Monte Alban. Still, she had a feeling that if she heard the name she'd remember.

It had been hot that summer, but both she and Emory had thrived on it.

"I love it here," he'd said. "I love the heat and the smell of the jungle and the mist that rises up off the mountains in the morning. I like the people, too. Most of the Indians in this area never mixed with the Spanish. They have their own customs, their own language, and they believe in the old ways." He'd looked around and almost to himself said, "If I ever decide to get lost, this is where I'd come."

Ariel's hands tightened around the framed photograph. "If I ever decide to get lost..."

Suddenly, clearly, she knew where Emory had gone. She knew that he was in Mexico.

For the first time since Emory had left, Ariel felt a sense of hope.

She planned the trip while she showered, shampooed and blow-dried her hair. Traveling would be difficult because her Spanish was limited to *gracias* and *buenos días*, but maybe she'd be able to hire a guide when she arrived. Maybe she'd even be able to find somebody here in Los Angeles.... Hair dryer in mid-air Ariel paused. Matt McKay spoke Spanish. He'd told her he did the night they'd driven out to the beach. She didn't know if he worked full-time for one company or if he freelanced, like she imagined private detectives did. If he did, maybe she could hire him to go to Mexico with her.

Ariel looked at herself in the mirror and ran a finger across her lips, remembering the feel of Matt's mouth on hers and the way she had responded to him. If Matt agreed to come with her they had to keep it a business arrangement. What had happened last night mustn't happen again.

She dressed in white jeans and a pink-and-white striped T-shirt and tied her hair back with a piece of pink yarn. Then she opened her suitcase and took out a small blue velvet bag. When she got to the bed she spilled its contents out onto the coverlet. There was a single strand of pearls with matching earrings, a jade ring that had been a present from her mother, several slender gold chains that Emory had given her, her mother's diamond earrings and the engagement ring Emory had given her mother when he'd asked her to marry him.

The sea-green emerald in the old-fashioned filigree setting had belonged to Emory's mother and to his grandmother before that. Ariel's mother had given it to her before she died. "It's yours now, darling," she'd said. "For you to wear to your wedding or to pass on to your son to give to his wife."

Ariel held the ring in the palm of her hand for a long moment before she put it in her pocket. Then with a sigh she put the other pieces of jewelry back into the blue velvet bag.

When she opened the bedroom door she smelled bacon frying and realized that for the first time in a long time she actually felt hungry.

She found Matt standing in front of the stove. He was wearing snug-fitting black jeans and a black T-shirt.

"Hi," he said over his shoulder when he saw her. "How do you feel?"

"Better than last night. It was awfully nice of you to..." She almost smiled. To what? Kiss the stuffing out of me? She swallowed a chuckle. "To bring me here," she finished. "I'm sorry about the weeps. That's not going to happen again."

Matt nodded. He liked the way she looked this morning, all scrubbed and clean, gray eyes clear, her cheeks slightly flushed. He wondered if her cheeks were flushed because she was embarrassed, and for a moment he had to restrain an urge to sweep her up into his arms. Instead, he said, "You're feeling better this morning?"

"Yes, because I..." She hesitated. "Matt, I know where Emory is."

He swung around. His expression changed, and his eyes went hard. "You've known all along, haven't you?"

"No." She looked surprised. "Of course not. I didn't know until this morning when I looked at the photograph again."

"The photograph?"

"Of mother and Emory and me."

"I don't understand."

"You asked me where it had been taken, and I told you it was in Peru. I lied, Matt. I don't know why, but I did. I'm sorry. The picture was taken in Mexico, and I'm sure that's where Emory is now."

Because he needed a minute to think, Matt turned back to the stove. He took the bacon out of the pan and put it on a paper towel to drain, then opened the oven and took out a stack of hotcakes.

"Sit down, Ariel." He indicated a chair by the window, and when she was seated, he brought the food over to the table and said, "What makes you think your step-father is in Mexico?"

"He said that's where he'd go if he ever wanted to get lost. I know it was a long time ago, Matt, but when I looked at the picture this morning I remembered everything about that summer—the heat and the flies and that I ate something I shouldn't have and got dysentery. I don't remember the names of any of the other people on the dig or the university that sponsored it, but I remember the musky damp smell of the jungle and the way the moon rose up over the mountains at night."

She put her hands flat on the table. "Emory said that it would be a good place to get lost, Matt. I don't know why he went away, but I know that's where he is."

"Mexico's a big country, Ariel. Do you remember where you and your mother and Emory were?"

She shook her head. "Not exactly."

"But you said—"

"I don't remember the name of the village, but I know it's somewhere between Oaxaca and Te... Tehuan-something and down near the coast. I know I could find it, Matt."

He drummed his fingers on the table, wondering if she'd known all along that Emory was in Mexico and had waited for the right moment to tell him. He wished he could trust her. He wanted to but . . .

"Matt?" She took a bite of bacon. "You're in security?"

"So?"

"I don't know whether you work for a company or if you sort of freelance. I mean, if you work for a company then what I'm thinking about probably won't work. But if you take different jobs, then . . ." She put her fork down. "I'd like to hire you to go to Mexico with me."

He stared at her, unable for a moment to take in what she'd said because he hadn't expected it to be this easy. He should have been elated. He'd gotten to know her just as he'd planned, and now she trusted him enough to lead him to Winston.

"I'll pay all of the expenses, of course," she said. "I don't know what the going rate is for the kind of work you do, but I'll pay whatever it is. I've got a savings account, and if it doesn't take us too long to find Emory I'll be all right. If not..." She reached in her pocket, took out the ring, and put it on the table in front of him. "This is worth a lot of money. You can keep it as security. If I run out of money before we find Emory, then the ring is yours."

Matt looked at her, then at the emerald.

"Was it a present from the actor?" he asked.

Ariel shook her head. "It was my mother's engagement ring from Emory. She gave it to me before she died." She looked down at her plate. "If you are not interested in going with me I can always hire a guide when I get there."

Matt stared down at the ring. "I can't take it," he said. He picked it up and reached across the table to hand it back to her.

But Ariel closed his fingers around it. "No." She shook her head. "If you have to use any of your own money during the trip, then the ring is yours. You can sell it when we return."

"Dammit, Ariel. I don't want your ring."

"Business is business, Matt. I insist. Otherwise, it's no deal."

A muscle jumped in his cheek. "All right," he said at last. "If I decide to go I'll put it in my safety deposit box until we return." He poured coffee into both of their cups and, trying to keep his voice casual, said, "But if you're not sure where in Mexico your stepfather is—"

"If I had a map I could show you the general area. I was only eleven when we were there, but mother and Emory talked about it a lot. I may have forgotten the exact location, but if I saw the names of some of the places I might remember." Ariel hesitated. "Look," she said, "it's okay if you don't want to go. All you know about me is what you've read in the newspapers and that hasn't always been flattering. I got a feeling that day in the playroom that you think I know more about Emory's disappearance than I'm saying. That I've been lying—"

"I didn't say that."

"Didn't you?" Ariel looked at him over the rim of her coffee cup. "I haven't been lying, Matt. I had no idea where Emory was until this morning when I looked at the photograph. I know that he's innocent of what he's being charged with, and I'm going to find him and prove it. If you don't want to go with me, it's okay. I'll understand."

"But I do want to go."

"Really?" She put the cup down. "It'll be all right about your job and everything?"

He nodded. "I'll have to make a few calls. When did you want to leave?"

"As soon as we can. Tomorrow or the next day." Ariel hesitated. "There's something else, Matt."

"What is it?"

"What happened last night ... between us, I mean ... musn't happen again. We'll be traveling together...." She took a deep breath. "You know what I mean."

A smile quirked the corner of Matt's mouth. "Yes, I know. And I agree that since this is a business undertaking we shouldn't mix business with pleasure."

"That's fine, Matt. I just wanted to make sure we understand each other."

"I'm sure we do," he said solemnly.

Maybe if she put a bag over her head and took to wearing tents instead of snug little T-shirts and jeans that covered her bottom like a second skin, he'd be able to keep his hands off her. Maybe.

He remembered how she'd felt in his arms last night, the way her lips had parted under his, how her nipples had hardened at his touch. His body tightened with the memory of it, and almost angrily he shoved away from the table and said, "Let me get a map."

"Here," Ariel said an hour later. She pointed to a section on the map that lay between Oaxaca and Tehuantepec. "Somewhere in here. Maybe further toward the isthmus." She frowned. "Or closer to the Gulf of Tehuantepec. I remember that the Gulf wasn't too far away."

"That's a hell of a lot of ground to cover."

Matt was right. Somehow this morning when she'd seen the picture she'd thought that finding Emory would be easy now that she suspected he was in Mexico. But it wasn't going to be easy.

"What I think we'll do," Matt said, "is fly to Acapulco and rent a car. From there we can head to Oaxaca and look around that area, then make our way down to Tehuantepec and hope that you'll spot something you recognize." He looked at Ariel. "Is that okay with you?"

"Yes. I don't see any other way to do it. When do you think we can leave?"

"I've got some things to clear up here. Today's Wednesday. We should be set by Sunday or Monday, so let's say we'll fly out of L.A. Monday morning."

"I can check into a hotel until then," Ariel said.

"No reason to do that." And when she started to shake her head, Matt said, "Look, Ariel, we're going to be traveling together for the next couple of weeks, so we might as well get used to each other. Last night happened, but it's over and done with. It won't happen again." He grinned at her. "At least not while I'm working for you."

Ariel smiled uncertainly.

"You were upset last night, that's all. You needed somebody to hang on to. I understood that, Ariel, but I'm afraid I got carried away. I apologize."

"That isn't necessary, Matt. Besides, I don't remember screaming for help." She held her hand out. "Friends?"

"Friends," he said, knowing he was lying.

Albert Quinlan's office on the tenth floor of the Continental Trust Investment Company befitted the president of the company. The carpet, a deep, expensive, yet conservative red, complemented the dark wood paneling, the big mahogany desk and the dark leather chairs.

A dapper man in his late fifties, Quinlan wore tailored suits and handmade shirts. He had married an Englishwoman his first year out of Harvard Law School, and though their marriage had been happy, they hadn't been blessed with children.

Matt had come to work for Continental eight years ago, and perhaps because Quinlan saw in him the son he might have had, he'd taken Matt under his presidential wing.

Now Quinlan stared unbelievingly at Matt and said, "You're what?" He smiled at the chunky man in the wrinkled suit in the chair next to Matt's and said, "I told you he'd do it."

"I'm impressed." Lieutenant Brezinski of the LAPD raised one heavy eyebrow. "How'd you pull it off, McKay?"

"I got to know her," Matt said. "She thinks I'm a security guard. She trusts me." He looked across the desk at Quinlan. "She's convinced that Winston is somewhere in southern Mexico."

"So she's known where he was all the time," Brezinski said.

"I don't think so." Matt shifted in his chair. "She was looking at a photograph of her mother and herself and Winston taken a long time ago in Mexico. She was just a kid then, but she seems to think she'll remember the place once we're there."

"Remember it!" Brezinski laughed. "Hell, she's known all along where Winston is. She's conning you, McKay, the same way you're conning her."

"I don't think so." Matt stood up and began to pace the room. "I thought the same thing at first, Lieutenant. But now I'm not so sure." He shoved his hands in his pockets. "This whole thing has been pretty hard on her. She—"

"Spare me the violins, pal. The little lady's in on this right along with her steppappy. She's probably been waiting to hear from him, or him from her. Now she's going to meet him, and once she does she'll dump you and they'll take off for South America or some place where they don't think the long arm of the LAPD can reach." Brezinski winked at Matt. "But you're going to be the long arm, McKay."

"What're you taking about?"

"I'll have a warrant drawn up today authorizing you to pick Winston up and bring him back to L.A. And I'll make one out for the dame, too."

"Her name is Ariel."

Brezinski smirked. "Ariel? Now isn't that cute. I guess you are getting to know her. How was she, pal? As good as she looks?"

Matt's lips tightened and his big hands curled into fists. He took a step toward the cop just as Quinlan jumped up from behind his desk. "Matthew!" he roared.

Matt stopped. In a voice shaking with anger, he said, "I don't know whether or not Ariel is in on this with Winston, Lieutenant. Chances are that she is. But that's no reason to assume that she's anything less than a lady."

"I'm sure the lieutenant didn't mean to imply that she wasn't a lady," Albert Quinlan said. "It was only a joke, Matt. Take it easy." He opened a gold cigarette case and reached for a cigarette. "Where's the girl now?"

Matt hesitated, then said, "At my place. I took her there last night." He glared at Brezinski. "She had nowhere else to go."

"Yeah, sure. We all know there aren't any hotels in L.A." Brezinski stood up. "I'll have the warrants ready tomorrow morning," he said to Matt. "You can pick them up in my office."

Matt looked at him, then at Quinlan. "I'm not sure I want to do this."

The lieutenant shrugged and with a sly smile said, "That's okay with me, McKay. I need a vacation. A couple of weeks in Mexico with a dish like Ariel Winston would be just the ticket."

"Damn you, Brezinski! If you weren't a cop—"

"But I am." The watery blue eyes were as cold as a winter sky. "Remember that, McKay. And remember that I'm working with Continental Trust on this because we want Winston just as badly as you do. Quinlan told me you were the man for the job, but if you don't think you can handle it then we'd better find somebody who can."

Matt faced the other man. "I'll be in your office tomorrow morning at ten. Have the warrants ready."

"They'll be ready." Brezinski flipped open his wallet, and Matt got a glimpse of the gold badge. "This is my card," he said, handing the card to Matt. "It's got the station number, the private line and my number at home. Call me when you find Winston. You need any help bringing him and the girl back, give me a call and I'll send somebody down to help you."

"I won't need any help."

"You got a gun?"

"Yes."

"Take it with you." Brezinski turned to Matt's boss. "Thanks for your help," he said. "The department appreciates it."

"And we appreciate what the police are doing. Emory Winston has taken a great deal of our money, and we want it back." Quinlan glanced toward Matt, then back to Lieutenant Brezinski. "Mr. McKay was in Army Intelligence before he finished his degree in finance and came to work for us. He's handled cases like this before. He's the best man for the job."

"Let's hope so." The policeman looked at Matt, but he didn't offer his hand.

When he'd gone Matt said, "I don't like him."

"Brezinski's all right. Maybe he's just been a cop too long." Quinlan studied Matt from behind his desk. "I was surprised to hear that the Winston woman is staying with you. You're not letting her get to you, are you, Matt?''

"Of course not. But she's been through a lot. I don't like having to lie to her.''

"And I don't like Winston's absconding with our money. He even took the film footage with him.'' Matt's boss put his elbows on the desk and leaned toward Matt. "You're the best man for this, but if you want to back out, now's the time to do it.''

"I don't want to back out.'' Matt stood up. "I'll go to Mexico with her. I'll find Winston, and I'll bring him back to face the criminal charges.''

"The woman, too, Matt. Don't forget the woman.''

Matt bit the inside of his cheek. "I won't forget her,'' he said.

Chapter 4

When the wheels of the DC-9 raced across the tarmac, Ariel clutched the armrest on either side of her seat.

"You don't like to fly?"

"Not very much," she said through clenched teeth.

Matt pried her fingers off the armrest between them and took her hand. "Close your eyes," he said. "I'll tell you when we're up."

She clung to his hand. He said, "Easy, easy now." And finally, "We're up, Ariel. You can open your eyes."

"It's just takeoffs and landings," she said apologetically. "I'm okay now that the plane is up." She darted a look out of the window. "What time do we get to Acapulco?"

"Three o'clock." He released her hand. "Ever been there before?"

Ariel shook her head. "Have you?"

"A couple of times. It's a beautiful place. If you want to stay for a couple of days, we can."

"I don't think so, Matt. We don't know how long it'll take me to find the place where I was with my family fifteen years ago."

"If you're worried about the money, don't be."

He felt guilty about taking her money, but she'd have been suspicious if he hadn't. He had no intention of using it, though; instead, he'd use the expense account money he'd received from both the bank and the LAPD. He couldn't very well tell her that, so he'd put both the ring and the money she had given him in his safety deposit box to give back to her when they returned. By that time Ariel would know that he wasn't a security man, that in reality he worked for the bank and, at least on this case, for the Los Angeles police.

He didn't want to think about how she'd feel when she found out he'd been lying to her.

It's just a case, Matt thought as he stared glumly out the window. He couldn't let himself get emotionally involved. He had to keep a part of himself, his personal feelings, out of this. Ariel was a beautiful young woman, and right now she was vulnerable. That combination could be tempting to a man. He'd have to be careful.

Matt glanced sideways at Ariel. She looked straight ahead, and he knew that in spite of the fact that she'd told him she was okay now that the plane was up, she wasn't comfortable. He wanted to hold her hand again. He wanted to turn the plane around and head back to L.A. No, not L.A. Somewhere else, where they could be alone and pretend that Emory Winston hadn't absconded with twenty-five million dollars, and that even if he had, it had nothing to do with them.

Two hours later Acapulco came into view, and Matt said, "We're almost there, Ariel. It's a beautiful sight. I want you to see it."

The plane dipped lower, and Ariel saw Acapulco Bay and the hotels, row upon row of them, rising tall and gleaming white in the sunlight. For a moment she forgot her fear and felt instead a tingle of excitement. As the plane circled for a landing, a parasailer, held aloft by a red-and-blue parachute, floated up and out over the bay.

"I'd like to do that," she said.

"I thought you didn't like flying."

"Maybe that kind I do." Ariel smiled at him. "Where are we staying in Acapulco?"

"At Las Brisas. It's a bungalow resort, and each unit comes complete with a stocked refrigerator and a private terrace. The one I booked has its own swimming pool. The surrounding grounds are so beautiful that somebody once said they look like the hanging gardens of Babylon. I hope we get a bungalow with a view."

"Bungalow?" Ariel raised her eyebrows. "Like in *one* bungalow?"

"It has two bedrooms." Matt shifted uncomfortably. "I thought we'd be more comfortable there than in a hotel and it's less expensive." It wasn't, of course, but she didn't have to know that. She needed to relax and Las Brisas was the place to do it, especially since the LAPD was picking up the tab.

Comfortable? She'd been sharing Matt's condo for almost a week, and while it had been reassuring not to be alone, she wouldn't have used the word comfortable. She'd been much too conscious of his male presence, of his sleeping in a room only a few steps from hers. Now they were going to share a bungalow, and she wasn't too sure how she felt about that.

"I know you want to get going as soon as we can," Matt said, "but you've been through a lot, Ariel. A few days relaxing in the sun would be good for you. The weather's going to get hotter the farther south we go, and we probably won't find the kind of accommodations we're getting in Acapulco. If you're not sure exactly where we're going, it might take us longer than you think."

"Maybe." She looked doubtful. "But the sooner we find Emory, the sooner we can clear this up." She glanced out the window again, and when she saw they were close to the ground, she squinched lower in her seat.

Without saying anything, Matt reached for her hand and held it tightly in his until they landed.

The heat hit them as soon as they stepped out of the plane. They passed through Immigration, then headed for the luggage carousel. While they waited, Matt looked around at the other passengers. They all had the same look of impatience. They were here, and they wanted to get their bags quickly and be on their way to whatever hotel they were going to. Women fanned themselves, and men tapped their feet and glared at the still-empty luggage belt. Matt, as impatient as everyone else, glanced around the room, smiling at a little boy who'd fallen asleep against his mother's carry-on bag. But when he saw a man watching Ariel, the smile faded.

The expression on the man's face was furtive, watchful, not the usual look of a man staring at an attractive woman.

Sensing Matt's eyes on him, he glanced away and reached into his jacket pocket for a cigarette.

"Here it comes." Ariel pointed to the carousel as the bags began to tumble out. By the time Matt turned around again, the man who'd been watching Ariel had disappeared.

Maybe it didn't mean anything. Maybe the guy who'd been eyeballing Ariel thought she was alone. A lot of guides hung around the airport in Acapulco trying to pick up customers. A lone woman was an obvious mark.

The thought struck Matt that maybe Brezinski had sent somebody down from L.A. to keep an eye on him and Ariel. But he shrugged the idea away and filed a description of the man away in his brain: Close to six feet tall. Bone thin. Angular face and olive skin. Could be Mexican, Greek or Italian.

He grabbed Ariel's suitcase, then his own, and headed with her toward the exit. He signaled for a taxi, and when one pulled up to the curb he helped Ariel inside. Just before he followed her in he glanced around. The tall thin man stood in the shade just outside the door, seemingly intent on other new arrivals.

But when the taxi started away from the curb Matt looked back. The tall man was watching them, and just for an instant his eyes met Matt's. Then he turned and quickly walked away.

The Las Brisas bungalows lay nestled against a hillside surrounded by gardens and rich green foliage. Purple mountains rose in the distance, and below them, the sea sparkled in the sunlight.

After Matt and Ariel checked in—as Mr. and Mrs. Matthew McKay—a smiling hotel employee by the name of Carlos put their bags in a Jeep with a pink-and-white-striped awning and headed down a flower-filled road past a cluster of bungalows to the one they'd been assigned.

"This one has a spectacular view," Carlos said as he led them down the path to the front door. "From here you can see the bay, the beach, everything. You have your own private swimming pool, and you are completely secluded from the rest of the bungalows.

"The refrigerator is stocked with a few essentials, and the bar has a variety of *refrescos*, soft drinks, as well as wine and liquor. The two bedrooms are just off the hall." He handed Matt the key, and to Ariel he said, *"Bienvenida*, welcome, *Señora* McKay. I hope you will enjoy your stay with us."

Señora McKay. When the young man left, Ariel said, "You shouldn't have done that, checked us in as husband and wife, I mean."

"I thought you'd be more comfortable that way." Matt smiled reassuringly as he gestured around the living room. "We've got a lot of space, Ariel. And if we're only going to be here for a day or two—"

"One day," she said firmly.

"I have to see about a rental car. I tried to arrange it from L.A., but the travel agent said there weren't any available at that moment for the length of time we wanted one. He thought there might be in a day or two, though." Matt put his hands on her shoulders. "We'll leave as soon as we can, Ariel. But meantime, why don't you take advantage of our being here and try to relax." He turned her around and pulled her along with him to the open French doors that led to their patio and the pool beyond.

Carlos had said they would be secluded here, and it was true. A high wall, covered by scarlet bougainvillea, surrounded the cottage. The only way anyone would be able to see them out there would be from a plane or a helicopter. They could swim naked if they wanted to.

That was a disturbing thought. Matt tried to turn his gaze away from the pool, but the vision of a moonlight swim with a nude Ariel played before his eyes, and his body tightened as it had the other night in his guest room.

He had to stop this before it started. It was bad enough that he'd fooled her into thinking he was a security man and that the only reason he'd come to Mexico was that she was paying him. He didn't want the extra guilt he'd feel if they made love.

Made love. Somehow he knew what making love with Ariel would be like, how soft her skin would feel against his, how warm her embrace would be. How…

Matt turned away. "I'm going to phone the car rental agency to see if they've had a cancellation," he said. "Maybe we can get a car right away."

But they couldn't. The young lady he spoke to said she was sorry, but so many people vacationed this late in the summer, and there were so many conventions in town, and most of them wanted rental cars for day trips. She would do her best though, and perhaps she'd be able to arrange a car in three or four days.

"No car yet," Matt said when Ariel came back into the living room. "I'll keep checking, though. Why don't you unpack and have a swim?"

"Yes, maybe I will." She hesitated. "Are you going to swim?"

"Not right now. I'll fix us a drink and a snack, and we can eat whenever you're ready."

Ariel hesitated. "You'll try the car agency again to-morrow, won't you?"

Matt nodded. "First think in the morning. I know how anxious you are to find your stepfather, Ariel. We'll leave Acapulco the minute we can. That's a promise."

When she turned away to go into one of the bed-rooms, Matt busied himself in the kitchen. There were fresh greens in the refrigerator, as well as sliced ham, salami and three kinds of cheese. He set about making a salad, but stopped when he heard Ariel say, "I'm going outside now."

"Fine. Everything'll be ready when—" He stopped and looked at her. She had on a turquoise-green suit that looked like it had been poured over her body. It clung to her breasts, curved in at her waist, and cut high up over her thighs. The high-heeled thong sandals made her long legs look even longer, and Matt had a sudden and clear vision of how they'd feel wrapped around his back.

He turned back to the sink. "I'm about finished here," he muttered. "I'm going in to take a shower."

"I won't be long."

"Take your time." He waited, his back to her until he heard her go out. Then he headed for the other bedroom where he stripped off his clothes and got into the shower. A cold shower. He gasped when the water streamed over his body, then gave himself a talking to. He and Ariel were going to be together for days, maybe weeks. He had to stop thinking about her in such a physical way. Okay, he'd face the fact that he wanted to make love to her. With her. God yes, *with* her. But that wouldn't be ethical, nor would it be fair to her.

He wasn't an adolescent kid who'd just discovered sex. He was a grown man. He could control his emotions. Couldn't he?

He switched off the shower and went back into the bedroom. By the time he was dressed, he heard the water running in Ariel's bathroom, and suddenly, vividly, he saw her there, her face raised, the water coursing over her small breasts, droplets clinging to the rosy peaks, rivulets trailing down her stomach....

Matt swore under his breath. Barefoot, his hair still damp from the shower, he went into the other room and poured himself three fingers of scotch. He drank it straight, then called himself all kinds of a fool and vowed not to let this get the best of him.

When Ariel came out of her room twenty minutes later he handed her a vodka and tonic and tried not to notice how feminine the off-the-shoulder white blouse made her look or how the blue shorts snugged in around her bottom.

"If you're not too tired maybe you'd like to see the divers tonight," he said.

Ariel nodded. "Yes, I'd love to see them."

"Things don't start until around ten, so we have plenty of time." He indicated the pool area, and not sure it was a good idea, said, "Let's take our drinks outside and watch the sunset."

He carried their drinks out and put them on a small round table between two pink-and-white candy-striped lounges.

"This is lovely," Ariel said when she settled back. "Right now I feel as though I could spend the rest of my life here."

Matt leaned back in his chair. "Yeah, me too." He took a slow sip of the drink he'd deliberately made weak. "Have you been back to Mexico? I mean since the time when you went with your mother and stepfather."

"Uh-huh. I spent a couple of weeks in Puerto Vallarta a few years ago. But I've never gone back down to the south where the dig was. I'm anxious to go back, Matt. I know the reason we're here is to find Emory, but I'm excited about seeing the country again, too."

"It's going to be hot."

"The car will be air-conditioned, won't it?"

"That's what the woman at the agency said. Let's hope it's true." He looked out at the sea. "Take a look at that," he said softly.

The radiant sky began to turn from a clear and brilliant blue to flamingo. The world caught fire, and everything became still. Puffs of white turned golden. Streaks of orange and pink spilled across the sky, and below, the sea, touched by the brilliance of all the colors, shimmered like a liquid rainbow.

"I've never seen such a sunset," Ariel whispered. "I'm glad we're here, Matt. I mean I'm glad we're both..." She blushed. "It's nice to have someone to share this with," she finished shyly.

In the glowing softness of the day she was heartbreakingly beautiful. He reached for her hand, and together they watched the brilliant sun sink quietly into the blue Pacific.

That night, at a little after ten, they went to the El Mirador Hotel. Matt ordered drinks, and they came in frosted goblets with gardenias floating on top. "It's gorgeous," Ariel said, "but what is it?"

"A couple kinds of rum with some mixed fruit juices." Matt grinned. "Guaranteed to be lethal." He touched his glass to hers and said, "Welcome to Acapulco."

The drink tasted cool, fruity and deceptively mild. Ariel had a hunch more than one would be her undoing, and she sipped slowly.

When the time came for the divers, they stood out on the terrace overlooking the sea and watched diver after diver leap from a precarious perch to the water below. It was as thrilling as anything Ariel had ever seen, and as terrifying.

When the diving finished, and the people who'd been watching moved away, Ariel became aware of the music. The rhythm, slow and smooth and Latin, floated out to the terrace from the room inside.

"Would you like to go in and dance for a while?" Matt asked.

"No, thank you. It's nice out here." The music was too seductive and the night too soft to be so dangerously close to Matt.

"Well, then." Matt held his arms out, and when Ariel hesitated, he said, "May I have this dance, *señorita*?"

Ariel hesitated, then stepped into his arms. They danced without speaking while she looked at his right shoulder instead of at him and tried to concentrate on the music instead of the warmth of his arms around her.

She didn't know very much Latin music, but the song the orchestra was playing seemed familiar. She hummed along with it, then suddenly began to laugh. "Do you recognize it?" she said to Matt. "They're playing a Latin version of 'As Time Goes By.'"

He listened for a moment. "By God, you're right." He started to laugh. Ariel laughed with him, and with their laughter the awkwardness faded.

They moved closer.

A breeze, soft as a child's whisper, drifted in from the sea. A golden slice of new moon shone overhead, and half a zillion stars winked down on them. Ariel rested her head against Matt's shoulder and breathed in the scent of jasmine and summer roses.

She gave herself up to the music and to the feel of Matt's arms around her and the brush of his lips against her hair.

She knew she should move away, that she should step back and break the spell of the music and the night. And him. Instead, when he urged her closer, she sighed and her body flowed with his.

She tilted her head, wanting to see his face in the moonlight, and when she did, he said, "Ariel?" and his mouth covered hers.

It was a gentle, warming kiss, and she stood, unresisting, in the circle of his arms. He sighed against her lips, moving her closer into his embrace as the kiss grew and deepened. Hands flat against his chest, she felt his heart beating as hard as her own.

His lips were firm, yet soft against hers, and the hand against her back urged her closer. Ariel clung to him, and they swayed together, oh so slowly, to the rhythm of the music and the call of their bodies, while heat, hot and insistent, kindled and spread.

He raised his mouth from hers. "Ariel," he whispered. "Oh, Ariel."

"We shouldn't—"

"I know." She trembled against him, and he felt an overwhelming tenderness. He kissed her, more gently this time, before he let her go.

They spoke little in the cab back to Las Brisas. Matt turned the light on as soon as they entered the bungalow, as though to dispel any pervading atmosphere of romance.

"I imagine you're tired," he said.

"Yes, I . . . yes, I am."

"I'm going to take a swim. I don't suppose you . . ."

"No," she said quickly. "No, I think I'll go to bed."

Matt nodded, and after a moment's hesitation said, "I'll see you in the morning." He took a step toward her, then stopped and murmured, "Good night, Ariel."

"Good night, Matt."

"Sleep well."

"You too." She turned away, but at the bedroom door she stopped and, looking back at him, said, "It was a lovely evening. Thank you."

She went in and closed the door, and stood in the darkness, trying to still all of the emotions his kiss had stirred. At last she went into the bathroom, where she undressed, and when she had put her nightgown on she came back into the darkness of the room and opened the drapes that covered the French doors.

As Ariel watched, she saw the movement of the water and knew that Matt was swimming. She was about to turn away when he hoisted himself up out of the pool and stood naked in the moonlight. His body, sleek and magnificent, looked as though it had been carved out of dark silver. He looked up at the stars, and she saw the elegant shape of his head, the width of his shoulders and chest, the narrow waist and hips, and the long lean lines of his legs.

As though sensing her presence, he turned toward her bedroom. He took a step, then stopped.

Ariel's breath clogged in her throat. She clutched the drapes with one hand, willing him to turn away, even as she willed him to come toward her.

He hesitated, poised as though unable to decide. Then he reached for a towel and wrapped it around his waist. And finally, after a heartbeat of time, he turned and crossed the patio to his own room.

Chapter 5

Matt lay in the middle of the too-big bed and looked up at the shadows cast by the ceiling fan going round and round. Though his body felt more relaxed after his swim, he couldn't sleep. Every time he closed his eyes the image of Ariel formed behind his lids, and he saw her as she had been tonight with the moonlight touching her hair and her face all soft from his kiss.

He put his arm across his eyes as though to blot her image away. He wanted, more than he'd ever wanted anything in his life, to make love to Ariel. But how could he do that and ever be able to face himself again? From the start he had lied to her and led her to believe he was her friend, when all the time he'd only been using her to get to her stepfather.

He pounded his fist against the mattress, angry that he had to be a part of an operation that he knew would eventually hurt her.

Brezinski thought Ariel was in on this with Winston. That's what he'd thought, too, at the beginning. Now he wasn't so sure. Maybe Emory had conned her into helping him. Maybe she'd gone along with whatever he'd planned without really knowing what she was doing. He remembered the man who'd been eyeballing Ariel at the airport, and it suddenly struck him that there might be more to this than anybody'd thought. Could the man at the airport have followed them from L.A.? Could he somehow be involved in all this? It didn't seem logical, yet the man had shown an unusual interest in Ariel.

Matt thumped his pillow and tried to get comfortable. He forced himself to lie still and take slow, even breaths. He willed himself not to think about Ariel. His eyes closed, and at last he felt himself drifting, drifting...

Then, in the silence of the night, he heard the tinkle of her music box. "Ariel," he whispered, and went to sleep with her name on his lips.

Three days passed before they were able to get a car.

"But it has no air-conditioning, *señor*," the young woman from the rental agency told Matt when she finally called.

Matt put his hand over the phone. "No air," he told Ariel. "What do you want to do? Wait for one that has it?"

"No." She shook her head. "We'd better take it."

She was anxious to leave, not just because she wanted to find Emory, but because Acapulco had become a dangerous place to be alone with Matt. The sun and the sea, the moonlit nights and soft Latin rhythms were an intoxicating combination.

That night, the scent of tropical flowers drifted in through the open French doors and as she lay listening to the soft roll of the ocean, she thought of Matt alone in his room and pictured him as she had seen him that night by the pool, his naked body silhouetted by the moon—tall, handsome and incredibly virile.

She remembered the way he had kissed her, and how his body had felt against hers. Her body warmed, and she lay naked, arms outstretched, and like Matt, tried to will herself to sleep.

Acapulco was an enchanting place, but she would be glad when they left. She had come to Mexico because of Emory. She must put aside whatever personal feelings she had and concentrate on finding him. Perhaps later, when he'd been found, when everything had been straightened out and his name had been cleared, she'd be able to sort out the way she felt about Matt McKay.

The temperature hit ninety-three the morning they left Acapulco. Matt had said it would be even hotter the further south they went, but it didn't seem possible that it could be any worse than this.

"Maybe we should have waited for an air-conditioned car," he said after they'd been on the road for two hours.

"I didn't mind the heat when I was here with my mother and Emory." Ariel fanned herself with the folded map. "I guess that's because I was younger then."

"Yeah, and now you're an old lady of twenty-six." Matt grinned at her. "Would you like to stop for something to eat?"

Ariel shook her head. "No, let's keep going." She studied the map, then looked at the guidebook they'd picked up in Acapulco. "We should be able to make it to Puerto Escondido this afternoon, and it doesn't look like it's very far from there to Oaxaca."

"It's less than two hundred miles," Matt said. "But we have to cross the Sierra Madre del Sur. Unless the road's in great condition it'll take us at least five or six hours. We'd better stay near Puerto Angel tonight and head for Oaxaca early in the morning." He smiled at Ariel. "I don't know what kind of accommodations we'll find, but I'm pretty sure there won't be anything like the hotels in Acapulco."

"I don't mind," Ariel said. "Just as long as the sheets are clean and the beach is close by. I can't think of anything better right now than a swim."

"Then we'll look for a place that's right on the beach." Matt slowed the car, then pulled off the road and stopped. After he'd studied the travel book for a minute, he said, "Let's try Zipolite. We should be there in a couple of hours." He reached in the back, opened the cooler he'd bought before they left Acapulco, and handed Ariel a cold drink.

She held it against her forehead before she took a swallow. "This'll cool me off." She clinked the can against Matt's. "Cheers," she said.

"*¡Salud!*" he corrected. "You've got to start learning Spanish."

"Okay," she said agreeably. "*¡Salud!*"

They didn't reach Puerto Angel until almost five. A fishing village and small-time port, it straggled around a bay guarded by two rocky headlands. A few kilometers farther on they came to Zipolite. A long, palm-fringed stretch of pale sand beach lay spread out before them, and through the open window Ariel could hear the pounding surf.

"This is wonderful," she said, "but I don't see any hotels."

"If we don't find anything, we can go back to Puerto Angel. I saw a motel there." Matt pointed further down the beach. "That looks like a restaurant. Maybe someone there will know where we can find a place to stay."

When they got closer, they saw what looked like six or seven cabanas down the beach from the restaurant, and a little further on toward the water, a row of hammocks slung between palm trees. Matt parked on the side of the road next to a beat-up Jeep and grinned at Ariel. "Ever slept in a hammock before?" he asked.

She shook her head and grinning back said, "Nope, but I suppose there's a first time for everything."

Matt reached for her hand. "I think I like you."

Ariel looked up at him and smiled. Her fingers curled around his, and she said, "And I like you, Matt. I'm so glad you decided to come with me. I'd have been lost without you."

The words, sincere and softly spoken clutched around his heart, and a surge of guilt unlike any he'd ever felt before made him wince. For the one-thousand-and-tenth time since he'd first met Ariel he told himself he had a job to do. *She* was the job; he couldn't let whatever he was beginning to feel for her make him forget that.

He let go of her hand and opened the door for her to enter the restaurant.

The restaurant, though rustic, looked clean. The woman behind the counter greeted them in accented English. There wasn't a hotel anywhere close by, she said, but the cabanas were for rent. "Five dollars a night," she said. "If you don't want a cabana you can rent a hammock and sleep outside for a dollar. The swimming is good, except for an occasional undertow. You can swim nude if you want to. Nobody around here minds."

"That's good to know." Matt smiled benignly at Ariel. "Isn't it, dear?"

Ariel blushed and looked away.

"We'll take a cabana," Matt said. And still smiling, added, "Two cabanas."

"Two?" The woman looked with raised eyebrows from Matt to Ariel, then shrugged. "That'll be ten dollars, *señor*. I serve dinner till nine and breakfast from seven on. How long will you be staying?"

"Just tonight. How's the highway to Oaxaca?"

"*Así así*, so-so. The road is narrow and mountainous, the curves are bad. It gets hotter when you leave the coast, so you might want to start right after breakfast."

"We will, thanks." He paid the woman, then said, "We'll be in for dinner in a little while."

Their side-by-side cabanas were sparse but clean. There were no screens on the paneless windows and no electric lights. A candle, with matches beside the candle holder, had been placed on the bedside table.

"Rustic," Matt said when he looked around.

"But it's clean and cool." Ariel smiled as she looked around. "I like it."

"You've come a long way from Beverly Hills," he said without thinking.

Her face sobered. "Yes, I have, haven't I?"

"I'm sorry. I didn't mean to say that."

"It's all right, Matt." She tossed her canvas bag onto the narrow bed. "I don't mind. Maybe it's time I turned my life around. I love Emory, and I've enjoyed working with him, but I'm tired of the Hollywood scene. I'd like to do something else, go somewhere else. When this is over, when I've found Emory and everything has been cleared up, maybe I'll come back here for a while." She forced a smile. "If my money runs out I can always hang a hammock between a couple of palm trees."

He wanted to say, Make it a hammock big enough for both of us, Ariel. But he didn't. Instead, he nodded and said, "This wouldn't be a bad place to get lost for a while. No telephones or television. No microwaves or frozen dinners. And the swimming pool goes on forever." He reached out and touched her hair. "Meet you at the beach in five minutes, Ariel. And remember, bathing suits are optional."

Ariel smiled when he left, then quickly opened her suitcase and pulled out a bathing suit.

The outdoor shower had been rigged up on the beach close to the cabanas. She stood under the lukewarm water for a full five minutes before she turned it off and headed down the sand toward the rolling waves.

"Hold on a minute," Matt called behind her. "The *señora* in the restaurant said there was an undertow."

Ariel nodded, and Matt watched as she headed down to the shoreline. She had on a strapless creamy-white suit that did great things for both her California tan and her figure. She waded in, then knee-deep turned back and said, "Come on. It's wonderful."

They swam for a long time. Ariel was a strong swimmer, but the waves were high and Matt stayed close. When she wanted to venture out too far he called her back in.

"You're acting like a husband," she sputtered.

"If I were your husband I'd make you behave," he teased. And to himself, thought, I'd haul you out of the water and carry you across the beach to our cabana. I'd strip the wet suit off you, Miss Ariel, and I'd lay you down and cover you with my body. I'd kiss your salty lips and your salty breasts and I'd take you so fiercely you'd—

"Catch me if you can," Ariel called, and when he looked up he saw her ten feet ahead of him, swimming parallel to the shore.

"I'd like to catch you," he muttered between clenched teeth.

"What? What did you say?"

"Nothing. Last one in buys the beer."

She laughed, then turned toward the shore, swimming strong, arms lifting and cutting back through the water in perfect strokes. When she touched bottom and began to run toward the beach, Matt slowed his strokes and watched her. The water clung to her legs and ran in rivulets off her body. She was a water sprite, Aphrodite rising from the sea, totally alluring from the top of her golden hair right down to her toes.

He wanted her as he'd never wanted a woman before.

There were a few other people in the restaurant early that evening. A group of men who looked like workers or fishermen crowded around one table stacked high with empty beer bottles. Sitting at a table near the door, a lone man looked up when they came in, then concentrated on the plate of shrimp in front of him. A corner table was occupied by a young Mexican couple. They held hands while they ate, and every few minutes the young man fed his girl a forkful of fish from his plate.

Ariel smiled at the young couple, and the Mexican girl smiled shyly back and unconsciously touched the shiny new band on the third finger of her left hand.

"Newlyweds," Ariel told Matt. "I wonder if they're staying here."

"If they are, I hope they've taken a cabana instead of a hammock." He looked at her over the handwritten menu. "Oysters?" he asked.

They ate their oysters with lime juice and hot sauce, and washed them down with ice cold beer. Then Matt ordered _huachinango_, which he said was red snapper. It was cooked with onions, tomatoes and chilies, and served with a crisp green salad and a basket of hot corn tortillas. Ariel declared the fish wonderful and attacked the plate in front of her with such enthusiasm that Matt laughed.

Her nose and cheeks were sunburned, and she'd tied her still-damp hair back into a ponytail. Dressed in denim shorts and a white shirt with rolled-up sleeves, she looked as though she'd never even heard of Beverly Hills.

Matt had a second beer, and when their plates were empty he ordered coffee. They sipped in companionable silence while they watched the sunset.

"It makes you wonder why anybody'd want to live in a city, doesn't it?" Ariel said. She glanced toward the other couple, who were looking at each other instead of at the sunset. The young husband whispered something to his wife. She blushed and put a finger against his lips. He kissed her finger, then slowly bit it. The girl's eyes widened then closed. When she opened them her husband pushed his chair back and come quickly around to help her with hers. He put his arm around her waist, and when they went out her head was against his shoulder.

"That's nice," Ariel said softly.

"Yes, it is."

"But a little sad."

"Sad? Why?"

"I don't know." Ariel hesitated. "I think the beginning of love is, somehow. I mean people start out with all sorts of wonderful expectations and then things happen. Life happens. There don't seem to be too many happy marriages anymore." She took a sip of her coffee. "Mother and Emory were happy, but they were an exception. They really loved each other, and they were a team. I mean, they liked being together, doing the same things. Emory was wonderful to her, to both of us. That last year when she was so ill he hardly ever left her side. He was patient and caring...." Her voice wobbled, and she waited a moment before she went on. "And...and afterward he did everything he could to make it easier for me. Somebody, maybe it was Fellini, wanted him to make a big picture in Europe. It was something that Emory would have loved to do. But he didn't. He stayed in Los Angeles with me because he knew I needed him."

She curled her hands around the cup. "He's not what they're saying he is, Matt. He's a good and decent man. I owe him so much, and I'm going to do everything I can to find him and help him."

"But if he did what they say—"

"He didn't," she said with certainty. "He couldn't have."

Darkness had settled in by the time Matt paid the check and they left the restaurant. They walked down to the shore and stood for a long time looking out at the sea without speaking. Matt thought about what Ariel had said about Emory. He didn't doubt either her sincerity or her love for her stepfather, but he found it hard to reconcile her image of Winston with the man who had absconded with millions of dollars.

He gazed down at her. She looked out at the water, her face pensive in the moonlight. She was so different than the woman he had imagined her to be. The longer he knew her the more he liked her. The thought of taking her back to stand trial beside Winston, of turning her over to Brezinski, chilled him. He wished he'd never gotten into this, had never heard of Emory Winston. But if he hadn't gotten involved he'd never have met Ariel. And that thought chilled him even more.

"It's so quiet," she said, breaking in on his ruminations. "All you can hear is the sound of the sea." She smiled at Matt. "In a strange way I like this even better than Acapulco."

"Yes, so do I."

"What time should we leave tomorrow?"

"Early. As soon as we've had breakfast."

"Then I guess we'd better get some sleep."

Matt nodded. But he was reluctant to go in. The night was soft, and the roll of the waves soothed his troubled thoughts. With a sigh he turned away and said, "I'll walk you to your cabana."

He didn't speak again until they were at her door. "I'd better step in and light the candle," he said. And when he had lighted it he stood for a moment looking at her, reluctant to leave. "I guess I'd better..."

She put her hand out. "Good night, Matt. Sleep well."

He nodded, then quickly turned away.

Ariel undressed in the shadowy darkness and lay down on the narrow bed. The only illumination was the streak of moonlight that came in through the open window. The only sound was from the sea and Matt's muted movements in the cabana next door. She was glad she'd asked him to come to Mexico with her because she wouldn't have wanted to make this trip alone, but he stirred feelings in her that she didn't want to feel, not when she had so many other things on her mind.

She moved restlessly on the narrow bed, and finally, because she was unable to sleep, she got up and put her bathing suit on. She hesitated, tempted to call out to Matt and ask him if he wanted to go with her. But she decided against it. The way she was beginning to feel about him, a moonlight swim with him wasn't a good idea.

The beach was quiet, and there was no one around when Ariel slipped out the door of her cabana. The sand, still warm from the day's sun, scrunched under her feet as she made her way down to the water. She waded out, waited for a wave, then took a breath and dove in it.

The water felt wonderful against her skin. She remembered what the *señora* in the restaurant had said about swimming nude. She'd never done that. Maybe one of these days she would.

She rolled over on her back and stared up at the starlit sky. The moon ducked behind a cloud, and a sudden breeze stirred the waves as she began to swim parallel to the beach. The breeze became brisker, and she found herself having to swim harder. As the waves swelled higher it became more difficult to keep abreast of them. Then she remembered all of the warnings she'd ever heard about not swimming alone at night and that the *señora* had said there was an occasional undertow.

Okay, Ariel told herself. Take it easy. You're a strong swimmer. You're used to rips, and you understand about undertows. So take it one stroke at a time. Don't think about *Jaws* or—

She went under, choked and fought her way to the surface. The undertow sucked at her legs. A wave slammed into her. She went under again and knew she was in trouble. When she came up she screamed, "Matt! Matt!" and headed for shore.

She was scared now, but she tried, with every ounce of her will, to curb the fear. Go with the current, she told herself, don't try to fight it. Easy. Easy.

The moon came out from behind the clouds. She saw the waves, higher now, and felt the terrible tug of water against her body. She had to get out of it. If she didn't...a wave crashed over her head, blinding her, gagging her. She fought her way out of it. And knew she was getting tired.

She tried to call out but seawater closed over her. She came up again and thought she heard an answering call. She saw Matt coming toward her and tried to swim toward him. Tried...

Matt grabbed her. "I've got you," he cried. "Take it easy. I'll get you in."

Ariel clutched him around his neck, but he knocked her hands away and with an arm across her chest began swimming toward shore. When she finally felt sand beneath her feet, she gasped, "I'm okay. I can walk."

But when she staggered, Matt picked her up and carried her up onto the beach. He put her down, and she clung to his arm.

"Thank you. That...that never happened to me before. I got caught in an undertow. I—"

"You damned little fool!" He swung her around. His fingers bit hard into her arms, and his face twisted with anger. "You could have drowned. What in the hell's the matter with you?"

Ariel tried to struggle out of his grasp, but he tightened his hold. "If I hadn't been awake.... If I hadn't heard you cry out...." He shook her. "Dammit, woman!" He held her away from him, then with a cry pulled her into his arms and kissed her.

His mouth was hard and angry against hers. She whispered a protest, but he only tightened his arms around her.

"Let me go," she whispered.

"No!" He pressed her close, and she realized he was naked. That frightened her, even as it excited her. She tried again to break away, but he held her still while his mouth ravaged hers.

A flame started in her midsection, caught and grew and spread, and suddenly she answered his kiss, her mouth as hungry as his. He cupped her bottom to bring her closer, and when she felt his arousal hard and strong against her wet body, the flame became a fire.

"Ariel," he moaned against her lips. Before she could protest he scooped her up in his arms and carried her toward the cabanas. He strode through his open door, then kicked it shut. "I want you," he said. "I've wanted you since the moment I saw you."

"Matt?" Her heart pounded so violently she could barely speak. "Matt, I—"

"You're cold," he whispered. "Let me warm you."

He carried her to the bed. For a moment he didn't speak, he only looked at her, then slowly he pulled the white suit down over her breasts and hips and tossed it aside.

Her body, touched by moonlight, was slender, yet sweetly curved. Her breasts were small and high. He touched them again, then ran his hand over the swell of her hips. "You're beautiful," he said breathlessly. "You're so beautiful, Ariel."

He kissed her again, more gently than he had on the beach, and lay down beside her.

"Matt ... Matt, wait. Please..." His naked body was close to hers. She hid her face against his throat and felt the tension in his body, the barely controlled desire. She raised her face to say, "No, I—" and he claimed her mouth.

"You're salty," he said against her lips. "And sweet."

Ariel tried to move away, but he tightened his arms around her. He reached for her breasts and held them poised against his lips before he flicked his tongue against one rigid peak. When he heard her soft moan of pleasure he closed his teeth around it to gently tug and moistly lap.

He moved one leg and slid it between hers. Her skin was smooth and cool against the heat of his arousal. He pressed upward, close, and she whispered, "Please, oh, please," and rocked against him.

He took her breast again, circling round and round with his tongue, then tasting as he'd wanted to taste for all these long days.

Her small, whimpering cries of pleasure drove him on. He came up over her, his body tight against hers, knowing he couldn't wait much longer to join his body to hers.

He raised himself over her and said, "Tell me, Ariel. Tell me you want this as much as I do."

"Oh, Matt. Don't you know that I do?"

He kissed her long and hard, pressing his mouth against hers, the way in only a moment more he would press his body against her body. With a low cry he moved swiftly, powerfully into her. Her softness closed around him, and he thought he would die with the pleasure of it.

"I've wanted this..." he whispered. "Oh, I've wanted this."

Ariel shuddered against him, then she arched her body up and tightened her hands on his shoulders, holding him, going with him.

She had never known such rapture. She was lost in it, in him, and she wanted this to go on forever, because nothing this good could ever happen again. All his now, she followed where he led, her body yielding, demanding, warming. And when she heard the rasp of his excitement she was exultant because she was pleasuring him. As he pleasured her.

He put his hands around and under her bottom to rock her closer, so close that she didn't know where her body ended and his began. She only knew that they were one now, moving closer and closer to that final peak of a feeling so strong it frightened her. And because it frightened her she tried to hold back. But when he kissed her again she became lost in the heat of his mouth and the hard beat of his body against hers.

She lifted herself to him, meeting him thrust for thrust, dizzy, disoriented, totally his while he carried her higher and higher on a wave of ecstasy unlike anything she'd ever known before. As though from a distance she heard her own pleadings and muted cries, her whispers of pleasure, her moans and her sighs. Then the night exploded, and wave after wave of passion lifted her so high that she would have tumbled off the edge of the world had she not been clinging to Matt.

He mingled his own cry with hers, then held her close, his heart racing as hers raced, her name a hoarse whisper as it left his lips.

"Oh, Matt," she said against his shoulder. "Matt."

He held her while her body trembled against his. He kissed her eyes, the side of her face, her mouth.

"I didn't know," she said at last. "I didn't know it could be like this."

He tightened his arms around her and remembered then how afraid he had been. He kissed the top of her head, and against her hair he said, "I heard you call, I ran out, Ariel, but the water was so dark. I couldn't see anything. I couldn't find you. If the moon hadn't come out from behind a cloud..." He rested his face against hers. "I was so afraid," he said. "If I had lost you . . ." He groaned and buried his face against her throat.

"I . . . I'm sorry, Matt."

He covered her mouth with his, and a shudder ran through his body. "I thought I'd lost you," he said. "Don't leave me now, Ariel. Stay here with me to-night."

"Somebody might—"

"Nobody will."

She sighed, then snuggled against his shoulder.

"Ariel," he said. "Oh, Ariel."

Chapter 6

Somewhere in the distance a donkey brayed. That was followed by the crowing of a rooster and a chorus of birdsong. Ariel sighed and moved closer to the comforting warmth of... of what? She opened one eye and saw Matt smiling down at her.

"Good morning," he said, and kissed her nose.

"Good..." She took a deep breath and opened both eyes. "Good morning."

"Did you sleep well?"

"Yes, thank you. Uh, what time is it?"

"Almost six. We'd better get a move on pretty soon."

"Yes, I suppose we should."

It struck her that this was a strangely polite conversation considering that their legs were entwined and that the hand that had been on her waist had moved up to her breast. "About last night..." she started to say.

"Yes?" He nuzzled her neck and began making interesting circles around her ear and on the tender skin behind.

"Matt?"

"Umm?"

"I think we should talk."

"Okay." He cupped her right breast and flicked his tongue across the nipple. "You talk and I'll listen."

"I think we should discuss..." A shiver ran through her body. "I mean about what happened..." A low moan escaped her lips.

"I'm a little busy right now, sweetheart." He scraped his teeth against the tender peak, then took it between his lips to suckle and tease.

"But we shouldn't..." Her body arched. "I mean our relationship isn't..." She laced her finger through his sleep-tousled hair. "We..."

He began to stroke her other breast. His fingertips brushed across the rigid pink tip, round and round in sensuous circles until she thought her body would burst with wanting him.

"We shouldn't what?" He shifted and began to stroke her body. His hand was warm against her skin as he moved it down over her belly to her thighs, down to the softness between her legs.

The breath caught in Ariel's throat. She said, "Matt, Matt, please," and tried to shift away. But he held her, gently soothing and teasing until she stopped resisting and gave way to the warmth that flooded through her body. She wanted him now as much as he wanted her. She raised her face for his hot, moist, deep kiss, a kiss that seemed to go on forever.

All the while he stroked her, stroked her until she was dizzy with wanting him, until her body arched against his hand and in frenzied need she began to touch him.

"Yes," Matt whispered against her lips. "Yes, like that." He closed his eyes and his body went taut with desire. The breath hissed in his throat, and his kiss grew more fiercely passionate. But only a moment passed before he said, "No more, Ariel, no more, my sweet, or I won't be able to wait."

He pulled her up over him, and a shiver of both fear and anticipation swept through her body when she felt the thrust of his maleness against her belly. Without conscious thought she moved against him, loving the feel of his body under hers. She ran her fingers through his chest hair and began to nuzzle and nip the side of his chest.

"You're salty," she murmured against his skin, and he felt the silky heat of her tongue licking him. When she reached for the nub of a nipple almost hidden by the thatch of curly hair, he groaned aloud. With the need to taste her, he raised her up so that could reach her breasts. Lifting his head, he brushed his face across their softness, feeling her shudder of pleasure with the scrape of his whiskers against the tender skin. Then he took one rosy peak between his teeth and held it there while he warmed and teased her with his tongue.

Almost past conscious thought, Ariel rubbed her body against his, murmuring his name over and over in a hunger she hadn't thought possible.

He tried to still her, because if he didn't, he wouldn't be able to wait. He brought her flat against him so that he could kiss her hungry mouth.

Ariel was all his now, malleable in his hands, her body hot and urgent against his, wanting him the way he wanted her, whimpering in her need, and sweet, so sweet. He couldn't wait, he had to take her now. Take her . . .

With a sharp cry Matt rolled her under him and joined his body to hers. The breath whooshed from her lips, and she cried, "Yes, oh yes."

Last night, she'd thought that nothing could ever be so wonderful again, but this was even more wonderful. She felt herself yearning, reaching, all his now as his body moved against hers. She wanted to tell him, but because there were no words to describe all that she was feeling, she lifted her body to his, offering herself. As she held her breast to his questing mouth while he suckled, her body moved wildly, passionately beneath his. She heard his anguished breathing, and his hands tightened on her hips as he thrust deep within her.

"Tell me," he whispered. "Tell me you like . . ."

"Oh, I do. Oh, Matt, I . . ." Hands flat against the small of his back, she pressed him closer as she began to spin out of control.

He knew. He said, "Yes, Ariel. Yes." Then, with a groan, he took her mouth, his tongue thrusting as his manhood thrust until she went wild beneath him, and together, clinging and close, they peaked the fiery crest of ecstasy.

Hearts racing, they held each other. Matt kissed her and smoothed the tangled hair off her face while her body trembled against his and small sighs escaped her parted lips.

His body had never felt so utterly at peace. It was as though all of the tension he'd ever known, all of the anger and stress, had somehow been eased. He cradled

Ariel in his arms and thought, it's you, my sweet. It's you who have made me feel this way.

In a little while, after their heartbeats had slowed and their bodies had rested, they got up. Matt went to the cabana door and looked out. "Nobody's around," he said. "I think we have time for a swim."

But when Ariel reached for her suit, he said, "No, don't put your suit on."

"But—"

"The beach is deserted, Ariel. There's no one to see us. We'll take a couple of towels and leave them near the shore so we'll have them when we come out." He put his hands on her shoulders. "It's something, one of the many somethings, I want to do with you. Please say yes."

She looked up at him, then slowly nodded.

Before she could change her mind Matt slung the towels over his shoulder and grabbed her hand. They ran, laughing, down to the beach, tossed the towels under a palm tree, then raced into the water.

It wasn't until Ariel dived under a wave that she remembered last night's fear. She came to the surface and reached for Matt.

"It's okay," he said. "We'll get out if you want to."

"No." Ariel shook her head. "I love ocean swimming. I can't let one bad experience scare me." She took his hand. "But stay close to me, will you?"

He put his arms around her. "I'll be right here, Ariel." For as long as you want me, he almost added.

They swam side by side, parallel to the beach, and when they were tired they floated on their backs and looked up at the sky. Her fear had disappeared, replaced by the joy of the salt water lapping over her body and the blue sky above her head.

"I wish we didn't have to leave," she said. "It's a paradise here."

"We could stay another day."

"I don't think we should."

"Why not? Will one day make that much difference? Besides, how often do you find paradise?" He rolled off his back and stood up so that he could pull her into his arms. "Last night was paradise," he murmured against her lips. "And so was this morning. I don't want it to end, Ariel. Let's give ourselves another day, another night." He kissed her salty lips. "Say it, Ariel. Say we'll stay."

Her mouth opened under his, and her arms came up to encircle his neck. He pressed her closer, and she felt him hard against her.

"Look what you do to me," he whispered. "I thought after this morning I'd be satisfied for a while. But now..." He cupped her bottom and brought her closer. "I want to make love with you again, Ariel. I want to fill you with this special part of me, to feel you close around me, warming me, holding me."

He raised her up and eased her legs around his hips so that he could feel her softness against his arousal. "What are you doing to me, Ariel?" he whispered. "What in the hell are you doing to me?"

He kissed her, then with a groan he let her go and began to stroke hard for the shore. When they reached the beach he wrapped the towel around her. "You're a sea nymph," he said as he pulled her to him. "I've fallen under your spell, Ariel, and I don't think I'll ever be the same again." Then he kissed her and led her to the cabana.

There were no preliminaries this time; he wanted her too badly to wait. He stretched his body over hers, and murmuring her name, he took her.

It was what she wanted, too, and she lifted her body to his with a glad cry, and they moved together, breaths mingling as they kissed, their bodies urgent and hungry. And when their cadence quickened, and in a strangled voice he whispered, "Now, Ariel?" she answered with a soft cry and arched her body to his as they tumbled over the brink of foreverness.

They ate a breakfast of tortillas filled with country cheese, and eggs laced with enough chili to make their eyes water. After breakfast they drove to the beach on the west side of Puerto Angel Bay. The water was calm and clear there, so they rented snorkeling gear and spent most of the day in the water.

In the late afternoon they sat in the shade of a thatched umbrella and watched the fishermen come in with their catch for the day, and the pelicans perched on wooden dock poles waiting for a scrap of fish. They bought cold beer from a stand on the beach, and when the man said, *"Su mujer es muy bonita, señor*, your woman is very pretty," Matt said, *"Gracias, señor,"* and smiled at Ariel.

"He called you my woman," Matt said when the man moved down the beach. "I like that." He took her hand and brought it to his lips.

The breath caught in her throat.

"I'd kiss you," he said, "but the pelicans are watching."

"Let 'em watch." Ariel put her hands on either side of his head, and bringing his face close to hers, she kissed him. "You taste like beer and sunlight," she said with a smile. "I like that."

And I like you, she thought. I like you so much it scares me. I feel things with you that I've never felt before. You look at me or touch me and my body catches fire. I can forget everything when I'm with you and that scares me, too.

This had been a day to get lost in. A day when she didn't have to think of anything except the sun and the sea and him. Tomorrow they would drive to Oaxaca, where their search for Emory would begin. But the rest of today and tonight belonged to her and to Matt.

The sun was setting when they drove back to Zipolite. Hand in hand they walked down to the water's edge and watched the sky turn from blue to flamingo and slowly fade to shadowed violet.

Ariel stared out across the expanse of sea to where the sun dipped low over the horizon. Her cheeks and nose were sunburned. In the last radiant rays her skin turned bronzy gold. He knew he'd never seen anyone as beautiful as she was. But it was more than that, for as she looked out across the sea there was a purity about her, an innocence in her expression that he knew was as real and as true as the sea.

A certainty came to Matt that Ariel could never be a part of anything that wasn't honest or decent. And with the certainty there came an easing of some of his guilt in not being totally honest with her, because he knew now that he would protect her against Emory and Brezinski, against the whole LAPD if he had to.

A feeling of tenderness so strong it almost brought tears to his eyes swept through Matt. He rested a hand on her sun-streaked hair, and when she turned to look up at him he felt as though his heart made a strange quivering movement.

He said, "Ariel?" and it was as though he'd spoken her name for the first time. He ran his fingers across her sunburned cheeks and brushed back the tousled bangs. He wanted to tell her how he felt, but because he couldn't he only said her name, "Ariel," again.

When they were back in the cabana he stripped her clothes off and laid her down on the narrow bed. "I want to make love to you," he said. "You don't have to do anything, only let me love you, Ariel."

Her wondrous gray eyes widened. "Matt," she whispered, his name trembling on her lips.

His gaze drank in every line of her body as he began to undress. Then he stood naked before her in the last light of the day. His muscled body was tanned and strong and ready. She lifted her arms, and he came down beside her.

For a little while Matt only held her close. He felt so much in this moment, so very much, and because he was afraid she could see all that he was feeling he pressed her head against the hollow of his shoulder. Her body was satin and silk against his, and when he knew he couldn't wait, he turned her face to his and kissed her, her eyes, her sunburned nose and her sweetly parted lips.

She sensed a subtle change in him that she didn't understand. There was more than passion in the way he held her now, a tenderness that she had not seen before. He rubbed his cheek against the softness of her breasts and whispered, "I love your breasts. I love it when you sigh and moan and I know I'm pleasing you." He swirled his tongue around one rosy nipple, and she murmured with pleasure. "Like that," he said. "Like that. It sets me on fire when you do that, Ariel."

He captured her hands and raised them back behind her head. Arching her body up he took a nipple between his lips and began to kiss and tease. When she moaned softly, he fastened his teeth around the tip as he scraped and tugged and lapped.

Ariel tightened her fingers on his shoulders. "No more," she pleaded. "It's too much, Matt. Darling..."

He trembled at the word.

"Oh, darling," she said again. "Oh, please."

He lifted his mouth from her breast and laid his head against her belly, then began to kiss and to taste his way down her body.

His tongue was warm and moist. Ariel's skin burned with each touch, every caress, and soon she began to tremble. She whispered Matt's name and tangled her fingers through his hair.

He went slowly across her flat belly, down over her hips. He parted her legs. Again and again he nipped and soothed the tender skin of her inner thighs.

"It's too much," she pleaded. "I can't bear it. I can't..."

His mouth moved, and fire surged through her body. She clasped his shoulders and tried to shift away from him.

But Matt held her, his hands on her hips, not letting her move away while his hungry mouth devoured her.

And still she protested, but her breath grew ragged and her words became a low moan of need. And when he felt her yield he let go of her hips and reached for her breasts and began to tease the already pebble-hard peaks.

Her gasps, her sweet moans of tortured pleasure, excited him as nothing ever had, and when her body began to quiver, he retreated for a moment to kiss her thighs, then returned to drive her closer and yet closer to the brink of madness.

When she cried out he gripped her hips, holding her, driving her on until her body shuddered and she pleaded, "No more. Oh, please...no more."

He soothed her to quietness with gentle kisses, then came up over her, and when their bodies were joined he said, "Again, Ariel. Again for me."

And when she did, his body shook and plunged over hers and he cried her name again and again.

They left Zipolite at dawn the next morning. Ariel looked back as they drove away, and because there was a look of sadness on her face, Matt said, in his best Bogart voice, "Don't worry, sweetheart. We'll always have Zipolite."

She smiled because his imitation of Bogart was so terrible. And though Zipolite wasn't as romantic a name as Paris, to her it was paradise, a place she would always remember. For it was here that she had begun to fall in love with Matt McKay.

She allowed the thought to form; she was falling in love with Matt. She hadn't planned on this. Love had come, unbidden and swift, and there wasn't anything she could do about it. She didn't know how Matt felt. Maybe when this was over, when they found Emory and left Mexico...

But she wouldn't think about that now.

The air grew hot and still almost as soon as they left the coast. Highway 175 over the Sierra Madre del Sur twisted and turned in torturous curves. They passed through small towns and villages, all with unpronounceable Indian names.

"There are nearly a million Indians in the state of Oaxaca," Matt told Ariel. "Something like seventeen different tribes and a lot of them don't speak Spanish. Some of them are descendants of the Zapotecs and Mixtecs, people who were here long before the Spanish came."

They passed a village of thatch-roofed houses. All of the women they saw were wearing *huipiles*, straight white Indian dresses that were elaborately embroidered around the neck and hem. "The ancestors of these people lived here as far back as 8000 B.C.," Matt said. "In 500 B.C. they started construction of Monte Alban."

"I remember that we went there. And to Mitla, too."

"Maybe now that we're here you'll remember more about the area."

But there was a part of Matt that wished she wouldn't remember anything, because he wasn't sure now that he wanted to find Emory Winston. He had set out to find Winston, and he'd deliberately used Ariel to do it. He wished he'd never heard of the man, because the closer they got to finding him, the guiltier he felt.

The last few days had been the most perfect of his life. He had never before experienced the kind of passion he'd experienced with Ariel. He had only to look at her to have his body catch fire. He hadn't imagined, even in his wildest fantasies, that anything could be like what he felt with her.

He knew that he was falling in love with her, and that scared him. He hadn't intended for this to happen, and there was a part of him that wished it hadn't. He'd lied to Ariel from the beginning, and the thought of what she would do, how she would feel when she found out, made his stomach tighten with dread.

He had to tell her, now before the affair went any further. What would he say? I'm not a security man after all, Ariel. I'm the vice president of Continental Trust, and I've got a warrant for your stepfather's arrest in my wallet.

And for her arrest.

Matt tightened his hands around the steering wheel. What was he going to do? How could he tell her? How could he watch the hurt and the anger rise in her eyes? And the hate.

He looked over at her, and when she smiled at him his heart twisted in his chest.

"It's awfully hot," she said. "Would you like a drink?"

"Yeah, a coke would be fine."

She reached in the back to get the cooler. "That's funny," she murmured.

"What?"

"That blue car has been behind us ever since we left Puerto Angel."

"This is the only highway to Oaxaca, Ariel." He slowed to take another torturous curve, and when the road straightened again he looked in the rearview mirror and saw the car as it came around the curve. He should have noticed it himself, and he would have if he hadn't been thinking of Ariel. He thought about the skinny guy who'd been watching her in the airport, and his face tightened.

He drove for a few minutes, and when he saw a lookout-point turnoff ahead he said, "Think I'll pull over so we can have one of those sandwiches the *señora* at the restaurant packed for us."

When he signaled for the turn, he checked the rear-view mirror again. The blue car slowed when he slowed, hesitated, then drove on past when Matt turned off. He tried to see the man in the other car, but all he got was the impression of a swarthy, mustachioed face.

When he pulled back onto the highway twenty minutes later, the only vehicle behind him was an old pickup truck with a bunch of kids riding in the back. But the next time he glanced in the mirror he saw the blue car behind the truck.

Chapter 7

For the next forty miles Matt tried to tell himself that maybe it was just a coincidence that the blue car was still behind him. He slowed down. Other cars passed, but not the blue one. He thought about the skinny guy at the airport in Acapulco, but the driver bore no resemblance to him, and Matt couldn't figure out what the connection might be.

He knew that speeding up would be risky on a road like this, but he didn't think he had any other choice. If the car really was following them he had to find a way to get rid of it before they reached Oaxaca.

"That blue car you told me about is still behind us," he said.

Ariel glanced behind them. "Two cars behind, Matt. You said this was the main highway to Oaxaca...." She looked startled. "But we stopped at the lookout point so the car should have been twenty minutes ahead of us. I don't understand. Why would anyone follow us?"

"I wish I knew, Ariel. It may only be a coincidence, but I don't like it." Matt covered her hand with his. "I'm going to try to lose him, honey, so I want you to hang on and be sure your seat belt is tight."

"Matt, I—"

"It'll be okay, Ariel." He took a deep breath and hit the gas pedal. The car leapt forward. He took the curve ahead fast, accelerated on the straightaway, took the next turn doing sixty, skidded hard, righted, and went flat out until the next sign indicated a series of corkscrew turns.

Ariel looked back. "We've lost him. There's no one behind..." She gasped. "No, there he is! What'll we do?"

Matt darted a glance in the rearview mirror and swore under his breath. He started into the first sharp curve, kept it steady into the second, and swerved around the third with his wheels spinning.

Ariel lurched against him, grasped his thigh, then straightened and looked behind her.

"Is he still behind us?" Matt wanted to know.

Ariel turned and in a voice tight with tension said, "No... Yes! He just rounded the last curve."

She wanted to beg Matt to slow down. If he missed a turn or lost control they'd either crash into the mountain or go over the side. When he shot around another turn she looked down a sheer three-thousand-foot drop to the nothingness below, and sucked in her breath. The only barriers here were occasional rocks the size of basketballs.

Ahead of him Matt could see a downward zigzag loop. He tightened his hands around the steering wheel. Taking it fast he sped around the side of the mountain, burned rubber and twisted into the second curve. The car rocked and swung hard toward the drop-off.

Ariel, fist to her mouth, smothered a scream.

The car righted. Matt took the next hook. "One more," he said under his breath, and prayed nobody was coming in the other direction. He veered into the curve. The car slid sideways and headed toward the embankment. The back tires screeched, but Matt hung on, knuckles white, fighting the wheel until the car steadied.

"It's okay," he managed to get out. He shot a quick look in the rearview mirror. "We—"

The blue car sped around the curve, skidded as Matt had skidded, shot toward the three-thousand-foot drop-off, smacked a rock, swerved, and headed into the side of the mountain.

It hit hard, the sound a grinding scream of metal in the clear mountain air.

Matt slowed, but when he saw another car come around the curve and stop, he accelerated again.

He let out the breath he'd been holding and looked at Ariel. Her face was porcelain white, her eyes wide with shock. "You all right?" he asked.

"I'm fine." Her voice cracked. She took a deep breath. "But let's not do that again for a while. Okay?"

"Okay." Matt tried to smile, but his lips felt stiff.

And until they reached the city of Oaxaca he drove as sedately as an old man out for a Sunday drive.

The towering Sierra Madre peaks surrounded the semitropical, five-thousand-foot-high Valley of Oaxaca. Twilight settled in as Matt headed to the central Plaza de Armas and arrived just as the old-fashioned globular streetlights went on.

"I like Oaxaca," he said, driving slowly around the plaza. "It's good to be back."

"I didn't know you'd been here before."

"I went to summer school here my first year in college. I'd learned Spanish on the streets of East L.A., but cleaned it up in Oaxaca. The following summer I went to a language school in Guadalajara."

"Where did you go to college? In the States, I mean."

"Stanford." Matt flexed his shoulders.

"You need a good back rub," Ariel told him as she rubbed his shoulders.

"I need something." He grinned at her. "How are you as a masseuse?"

"Play your cards right and maybe you'll find out." In a more serious voice she asked him the same question she'd been asking herself ever since the crash. "Do you think he was killed?"

"If he had his seat belt on, chances are he wasn't."

"I don't understand why he was following us."

"Neither do I, Ariel." He wondered then whether or not he should tell her about the skinny guy at the airport, but decided not to. Tonight he'd put in a call to Brezinski and find out whether or not the cop had put a tail on him. If Brezinski hadn't, then he'd start to worry.

They found a small hotel with a flower-filled courtyard and twisting stone steps that led up to their room on the second floor.

Matt hadn't asked Ariel if she wanted her own room, he'd simply signed the register as Mr. and Mrs. Matt McKay and asked for a room with a double bed.

"We'd better eat here tonight and try to get an early start tomorrow," he said when they were alone. There were sidewalk cafes and restaurants in the *portales*, the arched arcades surrounding the plaza, but he didn't think it was a good idea for them to be seen, not until he'd talked to Brezinski. He was pretty sure the man in the blue car wouldn't be up and walking any time soon, but he didn't want to take any chances.

When they went downstairs to the restaurant that opened on to the back garden of the hotel, Matt ordered chicken in *mole*, a sauce made from chilies, chocolate, pepper and cinnamon. It was hot and spicy, and they cooled their mouths with dark Mexican beer.

Ariel looked around, her face pensive. "It's all beginning to seem familiar," she said. "The food, the sound of the waiters speaking Spanish. I almost feel as though I've stepped back in time fifteen years."

"Do you remember being here in Oaxaca?"

"Not really, but we probably were because I do remember going to Monte Alban."

"Tomorrow we'll stop there and at Mitla, too, before we head on down to Tehuantepec."

"I'm sorry that I don't remember exactly where mother and Emory and I were, Matt. It's just that it was such a long time ago."

He reached across the table for her hand. "We've only just started, Ariel."

"But I hate having to drag you all around Mexico."

"You can drag me anywhere you want to." He smiled at her even though he felt tension tighten his body. He'd come to Mexico to find Emory Winston, and the sooner he found him, the better it would be for everybody. For Ariel? Yes, he told himself, for her, too. She had to find out for herself that her stepfather was a crook.

And when she does? he thought. What happens when she learns that I've used her to find him? How is she going to feel about me then? How will she feel when I slap a warrant on Emory and call in the Mexican police to help with the extradition?

And what of the warrant he carried for Ariel's arrest? How could he say, "I'm taking you back to L.A. to stand trial alongside your stepfather?"

Tell her who you are, a voice inside his head warned. Tell her now. His hand tightened around hers. He said, "Ariel..."

Just as she said, "There's something I want to say, Matt."

He bit his words back, and waited.

"I haven't really thanked you for coming with me. I suppose I could have managed alone, but it would have been awfully hard. I was scared to death today when the car followed us. I don't know what I would have done if I'd been alone. You've made me feel very taken care of, Matt. I—"

"Ariel..."

"No, let me finish." Her fingers curled around his. "There've been times in the last few weeks when I've felt very alone. But I don't feel like that anymore, Matt, not when I'm with you. I feel wonderful. The sky is bluer and the grass is greener." She squeezed his hand. "You saved my life in Zipolite, and more than that, you made me feel alive again. I'll never forget Zipolite or anything that happened there."

He looked into her eyes, and guilt, like a soggy black blanket, closed in on him. He wanted to tell her that he wasn't who she thought he was, that he had lied to her since the moment they'd met. But because he couldn't, he said, "I've fallen in love with you, Ariel."

That at least was the truth.

"Matt," she whispered. "Oh, Matt." And tears, like tiny diamonds, rose in her eyes.

"Whatever happens," he said, "remember that."

"What could happen?" A laugh bubbled from her lips. "We're in romantic Mexico, remember? We'll find Emory and everything will be straightened out." She ran her thumb across the back of his hand. "And someday we'll go back to Zipolite."

They talked little after that, and when they had finished dinner, Matt said, "I'm going outside to have a look around. Why don't you go up and have a shower?"

"I'll go with you."

"That might not be a good idea. I mean for the two of us not to be seen together."

"Because of the man in the blue car?" Her brows came together in a frown. "Is something the matter? Something you're not telling me?"

"I'm not sure, Ariel. I just think it's best that we're not seen together tonight. I won't be gone more than half an hour."

After he had taken her up to their room, he headed for the long distance office and placed a call to Los Angeles.

Lieutenant Brezinski came on the line, and Matt said, "This is McKay."

"Where are you?"

"In Oaxaca."

"Where the hell's that?"

"Southern Mexico."

"Still got the dame with you?"

Matt tightened his hand around the phone. "Yes, Miss Winston is with me."

"Got any idea where her stepfather is?"

"Not yet. Listen, Brezinski, I'm calling to find out if you sent anybody down to follow us."

"Follow you? What're you talking about?"

"I spotted somebody at the airport in Acapulco, and somebody else tailed us on the coast road today. You sure it wasn't one of your men?"

"You're damn right I'm sure."

Matt heard a match strike, then Brezinski inhaled and said, "Look, McKay, you're a professional. I didn't know that the first time we talked, but I've checked you out. There's no reason to spend the department's money to send somebody down to check on you. Who do you think it was?"

"I haven't a clue."

"Watch yourself."

"I will."

"Maybe you'd better contact the police so that when you find Winston you won't have any problem with them. Let 'em know who you are and check out your credentials. That way there won't be any problem when you bring him and the stepdaughter back."

"Lieutenant..." Matt hesitated. He didn't like Brezinski, yet he had a hunch the man was a good cop. "I'm pretty sure she isn't involved in this. I don't think she had anything to do with Winston's taking the money or any knowledge of what was going on. Somebody's following us, and I'm afraid she might be in some kind of danger. If I had my way I'd get her the hell out of here."

"Well, you don't have it your way, McKay. You've got a job to do, remember? So you hang in there or I *will* send one of my men down. You got it?"

"Yeah, I got it." When Matt slammed the phone down he swore at Brezinski, then at himself.

Then he left the booth and went back to Ariel.

He heard the music box when he opened the door of their room. It was on the nightstand next to the bed, and

Ariel, wearing a pale green chemise, was standing in front of the dresser brushing her hair. Without speaking, Matt crossed the room, took her in his arms and buried his face against the soft spill of her hair.

This was where he wanted her, here in the safety of his arms. He wanted to forget Emory Winston, Brezinski and the Continental Trust. He wondered as he held her what she would do if he said, Let's go away, Ariel. Let's forget about everything except the two of us. We'll get a plane out of here tomorrow morning for Guatemala City and from there to Rio. We'll lie on the beach all day and make love all night. We'll forget everything except this wonderful magic that's happening between us.

But Matt didn't say the words. He only held her and kissed her. And when he let her go he went in to take a shower.

She was sitting on the bed when he came back into the room with a towel wrapped around his waist. There was a quizzical expression on her face, and when he asked her what was the matter, she said, "I've just been wondering."

"What, Ariel?" He sat beside her on the bed.

"Did you graduate from Stanford?"

He nodded. "Got my master's there, too." He twisted a strand of her silky hair around his finger. "Why?"

"I don't know." She frowned. "It just seems strange, that's all."

"What does?"

"That you're a security guard. I don't mean to denigrate what you do, it isn't that, but with your education, it seems like a strange occupation." Ariel shrugged. "I just wondered about it, that's all."

Matt hesitated. Now, he thought. Tell her now! This is the time. Tell her who you really are and why you're in

Mexico with her. But he couldn't. Damn him to hell, he didn't want to see the way she'd look, the way she'd feel about him if he told her.

So he said, "I did a stretch in the Army. When I came out, things didn't work out the way I'd planned."

"I'm sorry, Matt. I shouldn't have asked. It isn't any of my business." She smoothed the still-damp hair back from his face, and because she was embarrassed that she'd asked about his job, she asked, "How about that massage? Wouldn't you like to soothe away all the tension from those tired muscles?"

Matt took a deep breath. Relieved that he didn't have to talk about his job, he grinned and said, "I'm all yours, Ariel."

With the towel still around him, he stretched out facedown on the bed. Ariel, kneeling beside him, ran her fingers lightly over his shoulders. She drizzled some of her hand lotion on his back and began to massage his shoulders and his neck.

He groaned, and she said, "Your muscles are tight, Matt. Try to relax."

She dug the heels of her palms into his shoulders, then squeezed with her fingers. He groaned again. "S'wonderful," he murmured.

"You've got nice shoulders," Ariel said.

Nice was an understatement. He had great shoulders, strong and wide and tanned to a warm golden brown. She ran the tips of her fingers lightly across his skin, and when his muscles quivered, a flare of excitement ran through her. She'd never done this with a man before, had never had a man lay so relaxed and almost naked, waiting for her touch.

She stroked down his spine to the edge of the towel. In a husky voice she said, "I can't really do a good job when you've got this around you." And tugged the towel away.

Matt turned his head and looked at her, but when she said, "No, close your eyes," he rested his head against his crossed arms and his eyes drifted closed.

She knelt over him and drizzled more lotion down the length of his body. She began at his shoulders and ran the palms of her hands slowly down both sides of his back. Then, because she couldn't get the leverage she wanted, she came up off her knees and straddled his back.

His breath woofed out, and he said, "Ariel?"

"Shh." She began to work on his shoulders, kneading them until he groaned aloud, and when he did she ran her hands along his sides, and shifting her body moved down so that she could rub the small of his back.

His skin grew warm beneath her hands. She spread her hands out over his hips, and under, and when he whispered her name she began to feather kisses up his spine.

She felt his excitement build, and that aroused her. The heat from his body spread to her loins. But when Matt made as though to turn she said, "No, Matt. Not yet, darling," and slid further down until she rested on his thighs.

She took the lotion again and squeezed dabs of it onto his buttocks, then kneaded the round firmness, warmed and soothed and teased until the heat from his body rose up to meld with hers.

The legs that held him began to tremble with need. She leaned over him and began to kiss the back of his neck and his shoulders. Then she kissed his ears and began to circle first one then the other with her tongue. His body began to tremble, and she whispered, "Soon, Matt.

Soon." And with a touch as light as a butterfly's wings she kissed and nibbled her way down his spine.

"No more," he rasped.

But she held him there. "Wait," she whispered against his skin. The kisses became nibbles, then tender bites that she soothed with her tongue. She said, "I love the taste of you. I love—"

With a low cry Matt shifted onto his back, and holding her so she wouldn't fall, he brought her around with him.

"Witch," he said hoarsely. "Don't you know how much I want you? I can't stand anymore. I want—"

Ariel kissed him. "No more massage?" she whispered against his lips.

"God, no! You touch me again and I won't be able to wait." He pulled the green chemise up, and when Ariel lifted her arms he yanked it over her head and brought her down into his arms and kissed her again. But only a moment passed before he gripped her waist and said, "Now!" and settled her over him.

Ariel gasped and softly moaned his name. Her eyes were luminous, her lips sweetly parted. Her warm moistness closed around him, and Matt felt overcome with pleasure. He tightened his hands on her waist. "Ariel," he murmured. And when she began to move in slow, circular motions against him, he whispered, "Yes, like that. Like that."

He bit down hard on his lower lip to keep from crying aloud while sensation after sensation flooded through his body. It was agony, it was ecstasy. It was unlike anything he'd ever before experienced. He reached for her breasts, and when he touched them she began to plead in incoherent whispers, "More, yes, like that, yes."

He couldn't get enough. He wanted this to go on and on until it was more than either of them could bear. He wanted to merge his body so completely with hers that she would always and forever bear the imprint of him somewhere deep inside.

Her movements were wild and untamed. Her body arched and her head went back, and he could feel the spill of her hair against his thighs. She whispered his name again and again and her body began to tremble.

His hands around her hips, he held her there while she sobbed her cry of completion. Still holding her, he rose to meet her frantic thrusts. And when his body exploded into a zillion pieces of wondrous light, he cried her name into the stillness of the room.

She lay over him, her body shaking with reaction. He cupped her face with his hands. He kissed her and said, "I love you, Ariel. No matter what happens, believe that I love you."

She clung to him. "And I love you, Matt," she whispered. "Always and forever. Only you."

He held her close. Above them the circular fan went round and round. The night grew still, and in a little while the curtains on the window stirred and a breeze cooled their heated bodies.

And finally, with her body resting on his and her cheek against his chest so that she could hear his heartbeat, Ariel slept.

But it was a long time before Matt did.

Chapter 8

Ariel stood on the summit of the grassy hill looking down upon the ancient city of Monte Alban. Because it was early in the morning there was no one else around, only Matt, who stood a short distance from her, his face pensive as he looked out upon the city the Zapotecs had built some seven hundred years before Christ.

The air was fresh and cool. A vagrant breeze swept in across the hill, bringing with it the scent of new grass and the shadow of an almost forgotten memory. Ariel shivered, and a feeling of déjà vu swept over her as she looked out at the remnants of a lost civilization.

It seemed to her she could see her mother and Emory and herself as a child on this very same spot. As though from a distance she heard her mother's voice say, "Just think, Ariel, families like ours lived here centuries ago. Little girls like you played there in the courtyard of the Grand Plaza."

Ariel hugged the memory to her. In the glare of the sun she tried to see the people from the past. She strained to hear the hum of their voices, the laughter and the music of the sacred drums. In her mind's eye she saw the priests in their feathered robes, the sweetmeat sellers and the children. She looked beyond to the ball court, the Building of the Dancers and the pyramid, and tears filled her eyes for those people, and for the mother she had lost. She wanted to relive the joy of that long-ago summer. She wanted to hear her mother's voice and feel once more the soft touch of her mother's hand upon her shoulder.

"What is it?" Matt asked.

"Memories. I was here with my mother and Emory. We stood on this exact spot, Matt, and I remember how excited I was and how I imagined that all of the children who'd once lived in Monte Alban were still here." She hugged her arms against the morning chill. "That was the last summer the three of us spent together."

Matt put his arms around her, and they stood together, there on the crest of the hill, looking down upon the ruins of a civilization.

After they left Monte Alban they drove to Mitla, a city that after the decline of Monte Alban had become one of the most important Zapotec centers.

"The Zapotecs named it Lyobaa, the tomb," Ariel told Matt, "and the Aztecs called it the Place of the Dead." She looked around and almost to herself said, "I know we're getting closer. I can feel it. If we can find the place in the photograph, then I know we'll find Emory." She linked her arm through Matt's. "I'm excited, Matt, but I'm scared, too, for Emory I mean. I'll be so glad to get everything straightened out so that he can come home again."

"What if he doesn't want to go home, Ariel?"

"But he will when he knows that we've come to help him, that he's not alone." She looked up at Matt. "I'm so glad you're with me. It'll mean a lot to Emory, too, to know that I haven't been alone, that you've been helping me. I can't wait until you meet him, Matt. I know you're going to like each other."

"Ariel—"

"He's a wonderful man. He's awfully talented, but I honestly think he'd rather be digging for artifacts than producing movies. And maybe after this is all over, when everything has been cleared up, that's what he'll do."

"What if it isn't cleared up?"

She looked at him, surprised, and said, "What do you mean?"

"What if he's guilty?" Matt chewed his bottom lip, knowing that she hadn't even considered that possibility. "A lot of people think he took the money, Ariel. If he did, he'll go to prison. I think it's time you faced that."

She glared at him. "Are you saying that Emory is guilty? That he's a thief?"

"I'm saying that it's a possibility."

"No, it isn't a possibility," she said angrily. "You don't know him. You don't know anything about this."

"Everybody in Hollywood knows about it. The money disappeared and so did your stepfather. Think about that, Ariel. Ask yourself why he ran away and what happened to the money." He took her hands. "I don't blame you for wanting to find him. I admire your sense of loyalty, but in this case I think it's misplaced."

"How dare you say a thing like that."

She tried to break free of his hands, but he held her. "I know he's been good to you, Ariel, but that doesn't mean he's not a crook. He—"

She broke away from him, her eyes blazing in anger. "If you felt like that why didn't you tell me before? Why did you come to Mexico with me?"

"Because I didn't want you to come alone. Because I wanted to be with you."

That at least was the truth. And now was the time to tell her the rest of it. But he knew that if he did she'd go on without him, and he couldn't let her do that, especially now when there was the possibility that somebody, for whatever reason, knew they were here and somebody was following them. Besides, he had a job to do and that job was to find Emory Winston.

But Matt knew that when he did, when he arrested Winston, that would be the end of any hope that he and Ariel might have of a life together.

Matt's insides clenched in pain. He couldn't face the thought of losing her. The days and the nights they'd spent together had been the happiest he'd ever known. There'd been other women in his life, but with none of them had he experienced what he'd felt with Ariel. Every time they made love it was like the first time.

He loved her, and if he could have his way they'd find a *padre* and get married today. And once they were married he'd never let her go.

But first he had to deal with the matter of her stepfather, and so he said, "Look, maybe I'm wrong about him. I hope I am, but even if I'm not it doesn't have anything to do with you and me, Ariel, with what we feel for each other. Whatever happens nothing will change that."

He put his arms around her, but her body felt stiff and unyielding in his embrace.

When an elderly man in worn but clean clothes approached them and asked if he could guide them around the ruins, Matt readily agreed.

But when the sun grew hot overhead, Matt paid the man. "It's going to be a scorcher today," he said to Ariel. "We'd better start down toward Tehuantepec."

They spoke very little in the car. The conversation at Mitla had sobered Ariel. These last few days, because of her growing attraction to Matt, she had allowed herself to put aside her concern for Emory. She'd gotten lost in all of the new feelings awakening in her body. Every time Matt looked at her or touched her she felt as though her bones were melting. Last night . . . Hot color flooded her face and she turned to look out the window so Matt wouldn't see her.

For as long as she could remember she'd always been in control of her emotions. But she hadn't been in control last night. She'd been wildly uninhibited, free to express her sensuality, to love and know that she was loved in return. Now she was afraid. Suddenly she wasn't sure of Matt.

Last night she had questioned his being a security officer because it had seemed strange to her that with a master's from Stanford he'd chosen that particular line of work.

She felt a stirring of disquiet. She knew so little about Matt. The first time she'd met him she'd been too emotionally frazzled to think clearly. He'd persuaded her to have dinner with him, and she remembered now that he had asked her questions about Emory. She'd thought he'd only asked because he was curious, as so many people were. Now she wondered if it had been more than curiosity that had prompted the questions.

When she'd asked Matt to accompany her to Mexico he'd agreed. Too quickly? she wondered. Had he had his own reasons for coming with her?

Ariel tried to shake the troublesome thoughts away. Matt had said he loved her. She couldn't believe that everything that had happened between them had been calculated. Matt didn't know Emory. Once he did, it would be different. He'd see what kind of a man Emory was, he'd understand why she wanted to help him.

She didn't like this silence between them, so she put her hand over the hand on the steering wheel and said, "Don't you think it's about time to stop for lunch?"

Matt nodded, more relieved than he could say that the tension between them was easing. "I was just going to suggest it," he said. "I thought we'd stay in Tehuantepec tonight. Tomorrow we'll begin cruising the different archaeological areas to see if there's anything you remember."

"I wish I could think of the name of a town or a village, something that would give me a clue as to where we were. The rate I'm going, it will take us weeks to find Emory."

"We've got all the time in the world, Ariel. Don't worry about it."

All the time in the world? Again she felt a niggle of doubt. "What about your job?" She watched his face. "Don't you have to be back at a certain time, Matt?"

"No, I, uh . . . I sort of freelance, Ariel. I mean I work for different companies. I'm not on any special schedule." He forced a smile. "Don't worry about it, okay?"

They made Tehuantepec while it was still daylight and found a hotel off the main plaza. After they checked into the twin-bedded room they went out to dinner, then rode around the town on a *motocarro*, a three-wheeled buggy. The driver sat in the front, and Matt and Ariel stood behind him on a small platform, holding on to a rail. It was a strange means of transportation, a clumsy, oversized chariot, but it was fun seeing the town in this way.

The younger women of Tehuantepec were dressed in modern clothes, but most of the older women, Ariel noticed, still wore the *huipiles* and the beautiful flower-embroidered skirts.

"I like it here," Ariel said. "It's an interesting city."

"Once upon a time it was a boomtown. The Mexicans built a railway across the isthmus at the turn of the century to link the Gulf of Mexico, the Atlantic and the Caribbean with the Pacific. But the Mexican Revolution came along, and then the Panama Canal was built." Matt shook his head. "That ended their hope of prosperity." He looked at Ariel. "Does the town seem at all familiar?"

"I'm afraid not. We might have been here, but I don't really remember."

When the *motocarro* let them off in front of their hotel, they went up to their room, and when they opened the door Matt switched on the overhead fan.

"It's hot in here," he said. "I was going to suggest we sleep in one of the twin beds, but I guess it'd be better to shove the beds together."

"No, leave them the way they are." Ariel looked at him, then quickly away. "I mean it's...it's so hot. It's too hot to... I mean we'll be cooler alone."

Matt raised an eyebrow. "Whatever you want," he said, and knew that she was still upset from their conversation in Mitla after all.

There wasn't a hell of a lot he could do about it. They were getting closer now, and the closer they came to finding Emory Winston the closer they came to Ariel's finding out why he'd really come to Mexico.

He took a shower in a thin drizzle of tepid water and dried himself with a worn towel that he wrapped around his waist when he came out of the bathroom. It had seemed natural to walk around naked in front of Ariel before, but it didn't now.

He lay on one of the narrow beds and waited for her when she went in to take her shower. He hated this awkwardness between them and wondered if he should try to talk to her. Or make love to her.

She wore a long white cotton gown when she came out of the shower. Before he had a chance to speak, she said, "I'm awfully tired tonight, Matt. I guess it's the heat."

"Yeah, that's probably it."

She sat down on the other bed. She looked at him uncertainly, then said, "Well . . . good night."

He reached out to snap the light off. "Good night, Ariel, sleep well."

He heard the springs squeak and knew she'd lain down, but after that she was so quiet he couldn't even hear her breathing. He lay still, hands clenched to his sides because he wanted to go to her. But strangely, his wanting to go to her didn't have as much to do with passion as it did with wanting to be close to her. He wanted to tell her that it didn't matter who he was or why he'd come to Mexico, that he loved her and that was all that mattered.

He lay looking up at the circular fan going round and round, then at last heard her sigh and knew that she'd gone to sleep.

But he didn't, not for a very long time. He turned on his side, and by the streetlight that shone in through the window, he watched her. What's going to happen to us when I find your stepfather? he asked himself. Will you still love me? Will you believe that I love you?

"Ariel," he whispered into the quiet of the night. And at last, with her name on his lips, he drifted to sleep.

They spent the next two days driving to all the little towns near Tehuantepec. They went through Jalapa and Juchitán, then up as far as Ciudad Ixtepec before they cut over to Tequisistian and Nejapa. They drove down rutted dirt roads and through cobblestone villages. They passed pineapple and coffee plantations and fields of sugarcane. The car was a sauna on wheels. The flies and mosquitoes banded together to attack every time they stepped outside of a hotel or the car.

Ariel wore a *huipil* and leather sandals to try to keep cool, but nothing helped the heat.

"It's so still," she said one afternoon when they stopped in a palm-thatched restaurant for a cold drink. She fanned herself with a palm frond fan and looked out at the countryside. "There isn't even the breath of a breeze."

"Hurricane season," Matt said.

"They have hurricanes here?"

"Sure. This area can get it from both directions, down through the Gulf of Mexico and up from the Pacific. The isthmus is Mexico's narrowest point, and it's all low-lying land. The hurricane that swept through here a lot of years ago just about wiped out everything in its path." He gestured at the restaurant they were sitting in. "You've seen some of the houses in the villages we've driven through. They're built just about like this. Can you imagine what a hundred and thirty mile an hour wind would do?'' He batted a mosquito out of the way. ''But at least communications are better today. Just about everybody has a radio or a television, so at least they know when a storm is coming.''

''I remember it being hot when I was here,'' Ariel said. ''But not this hot. Where are we going this afternoon?''

Matt spread the archaeological map out on the table. ''There's a place called Guiengola that we haven't checked out. It was a fortress city where the Zapotecs fought off the Aztecs. There are the remains of a pyramid and a few smaller buildings, and I think we ought to take a look at it. It says here the ruins are about halfway up the mountain and go all the way to the top where the Chontal Indians raise corn. There's a town not too far from it, and maybe we'll find a place to stay there.''

When they had checked out of the hotel in Tehuantepec that morning, Matt had made up his mind there weren't going to be any more twin beds. He'd ask for *una cama matrimonial*, a marriage bed, the next place they stayed, and he wouldn't settle for anything less.

The tension between them had eased, but they hadn't made love. ''It's too warm,'' Ariel had said. ''The bed is uncomfortable.'' And last night she'd said, ''I wish we were back in Zipolite.''

So did he. If they didn't find Winston in a couple of days that's what he was going to suggest. They could spend a few days on the beach, then come back here and resume their search. She needed the break because the heat was getting to her. She wasn't eating properly, and she'd lost weight.

But that wasn't the real reason Matt wanted to go back to the beach. He and Ariel had found something special in Zipolite, and he wanted to recapture it. He wanted to hold Ariel in his arms again while they listened to the slow roll of the ocean waves. He wanted to hear her whisper his name in the stillness of the night, and feel her close to him.

When they had finished their drinks they got back in the car and headed toward Guiengola. Forty-five minutes later they saw a sign indicating the ruins. They turned off onto a narrow dirt road and drove for little over a mile before they came to another sign. Matt parked the car. "This is it," he said.

Ariel looked around. "Now we climb the mountain." She sighed and got out of the car.

"'Fraid so." Matt took her arm. "Maybe there'll be more of a breeze farther up."

"Don't count on it." She looked around. It seemed greener here. Not as dusty and dry as the ground they'd covered the last few days, and the air seemed somehow fresher in spite of the heat.

When they stopped part way up, Matt said, "I should have brought the thermos of water along."

"Or a cold beer." Ariel swiped a hand across her face. "How much farther do you think it is?"

Matt shaded his eyes with his hand. "I can see the remnants of a wall. The guidebook says that when it was built it was ten feet high and six feet thick and it surrounded the entire mountain. I guess that's what kept the Aztecs out." He reached his hand out to her. "Come on," he said, "let's get it over with."

They climbed the rest of the way in silence. When they got to the remains of the wall they saw there were two more walls, like inner lines of defense, then a short flight of crumbled stairs that led into a plaza that was surrounded by pyramidal ruins and temple platforms.

"You can see the river from the ball court," Ariel said. "It…" She looked at Matt and her eyes opened wide. "I remember, Matt! This is the dig we were on. The tents were just beyond the wall, and we brought food in from . . . from a village called Magdalena ." She grabbed his arm. "I know this is where we were, Matt. I know it."

"You're sure?"

"Yes. And if this is the dig, it means that Emory is somewhere close by. Maybe in Magdalena."

Matt pulled out the map. He studied it for a minute or two, then said, "Yes, here it is. But it's only a village, Ariel. I doubt there's even a hotel there."

"But let's try. All right?"

Matt saw the excitement in her face. He nodded and said, "Sure, we'll give it a try." And tried to quell his own feelings of dread.

When they reached the car Matt consulted the map before he got back onto the main road and headed for the village of Magdalena.

He was so occupied with his own thoughts that he didn't see the small gray Volkswagen that pulled out of a stand of trees and began to follow them.

Chapter 9

The Hotel Jacaranda sat back from the road among a stand of mango trees. Crotons, hibiscus and wild orchids grew along the path leading to the entrance. Purple bougainvillea covered one wall all the way up to the red-tiled roof.

Once inside, Matt and Ariel were greeted by a rotund man with multitudinous chins and warm brown eyes. He introduced himself as *Señor* Alfredo Melendez, and when Matt told him they'd like a double room, he said, "We have a nice double on the second floor, *Señor*. There are not too many people who come to the ruins of Guiengola anymore. There used to be though, many years ago, archaeologists as well as tourists."

"I was here fifteen years ago," Ariel said. "I came on a dig with my mother and stepfather."

"And now you've come back." *Señor* Melendez smiled. "Are your parents with you or is it just you and your husband?"

"Just the two of us," Matt said, "but we're hoping to find my wife's stepfather here." He looked at Ariel. "May I have Emory's picture, dear?"

She hesitated, then opened her shoulder bag and took Emory's picture out of her wallet.

"We're pretty sure he's in the area," Matt said while *Señor* Melendez studied the picture. "Have you seen him?"

Señor Melendez studied the photograph. "I don't think so, *Señor* McKay, but I've been away for several months. I returned only yesterday from Mexico City. My brother has been taking my place while I've been gone."

"Maybe we could speak to him."

"He's in Oaxaca for a few days, but he'll be back by the end of the week. You might ask the waiter in the dining room, though." He smiled at Ariel. "The dining room here at the hotel is the only restaurant in the village, *señora*, so many people passing through our village eat at the hotel. We are open for breakfast and for the *comida*, which we serve from one-thirty until five. How long will you be with us?"

"Three or four days," Matt said.

"*Muy bien, señor.*" Melendez handed Matt the key. "Your room is number six. I am sure everything is in order."

"In order, but hot," Ariel said when they opened the door. "I'll never complain about cool and cloudy California weather again. I almost wish there would be a hurricane. Maybe it'd cool things off."

"A shower will help." Matt, pleased to see that there was a double bed in the room, put their suitcases on a bench. "It's almost four," he said. "Why don't we take a shower and have something to eat?"

Ariel nodded. "And after we eat we can have a look around."

"Sure. Whatever you want."

She opened her suitcase and took out the photograph that had been taken fifteen years before. "I'll take this photograph, too. Somebody might recognize the location."

"Yeah, that's a good idea."

But there was a part of Matt that hoped no one would recognize Emory Winston or the place in the photograph. Winston was a crook, and he should be prosecuted, but the thought of what it would do to Ariel when he arrested the man chilled him.

So he felt a sense of relief when the waiter, after he had studied both pictures, said, "No, *señor*. I do not know this man."

They ate fried fish that the waiter told them had been caught in Salina Cruz that morning, along with a plate of rice and beans, and after they had eaten they got back in the car and drove the few blocks down to the center of the village. With Emory's photograph in hand they went to the barber shop, the bakery and a mechanic shop. Nobody remembered seeing Winston. But in the small miscellaneous store in front of the grassy central plaza, the woman behind the counter said, "*Pues, si*, the American comes in once every week or so to buy groceries."

"Do you know where he lives?" Ariel asked excitedly. "I'm his daughter. I'm trying to find him."

"No, *señora*. I am sorry, but I have no idea. Many people come here to shop from the small ranchos or the neighboring villages. The next time he comes in, I'll be glad to tell him that you and the *señor* are looking for him."

"When was the last time he was here?" Matt asked.

"Two or three days ago, *señor*."

Matt looked at Ariel. "If we don't find him in the next couple of days, we'll do a stakeout."

"A stakeout?" Her eyebrows shot up. "You sound like a cop."

"Maybe I watch too many shoot-'em-ups." Matt forced a smile. "I meant to say that if we don't find him by the end of the week, either you or I will hang around the store and wait for him to show up."

After he had thanked the woman, he took Ariel's arm and said, "Let's drive around and see if anything else looks familiar to you."

But nothing did. They stopped in several villages and went into other stores. The people in this region, mostly Indians and not used to outsiders, were coolly polite. They looked at both photographs, their faces stoic, and in every case they shook their heads, then turned back to what they'd been doing before they'd been interrupted.

Finally Matt and Ariel drove down to Salina Cruz. Armed with the two photographs they went from store to store, restaurant to restaurant, but no one recognized Emory Winston.

When they left Salina Cruz, they drove the short distance to San Mateo and stopped for a cold beer in an outdoor restaurant overlooking the Gulf of Tehuantepec.

They had come so far, Ariel thought as she looked out over the water. So much had changed in her life since Emory's disappearance. She wasn't the same woman that had started out only a few weeks ago from Los Angeles. And she knew, somehow, that she would never be the same again, for Matt had changed her. She had fallen in love for the first time in her life, but there was an edge of sadness in the love she couldn't dispel.

She had no idea what the next few months would bring. She only knew there would be terrible problems to face when Emory went back to Los Angeles. He might be arrested. There might be a trial. She had to start thinking of him now and put all of her mixed-up feelings for Matt aside until this was over.

She turned to look at Matt. In the dusky light of the setting sun his skin had turned the color of old bronze. His face, so strong that at times it seemed almost harsh, was softened by a smile as he watched a young boy proudly hold aloft a prize fish.

His white shirt was open, revealing his tanned chest and the V-shaped thatch of hair that narrowed at the waist of his khaki shorts. Her gaze slipped lower, to his muscular thighs, and for a moment a wave of hot desire ran like a fever through her body. She held the icy can of beer to her throat in a vain attempt to cool the passion that had begun to throb. She tried to tell herself that she was still angry with Matt because he didn't believe, as she did, in her stepfather's innocence. But all she could think about was Matt and the way she felt when he made love to her.

It was dark by the time they got back to Magdalena. In the shadow of the trees the hotel seemed cooler than it had earlier, and when they went up to their room they saw that a maid had turned back the bed and that the overhead circular fan was on.

"It doesn't seem as hot tonight as it's been," Matt said. And because he was still unsure of her feelings, he added, "You look tired, Ariel."

"I am." She tossed her shoulder bag on the foot of the bed. "But I'll feel better after I've had a shower."

"Then why don't you go first?"

PLAY THE

scratch-off game
and get as many as
SIX FREE GIFTS...

HOW TO PLAY:

1. With a coin, carefully scratch off the silver area at right. Then check your number against the chart below it to find out which gifts you're eligible to receive.

2. You'll receive brand-new Silhouette Intimate Moments® novels and possibly other gifts—ABSOLUTELY FREE! Send back this card and we'll promptly send you the free books and gifts you qualify for!

3. We're betting you'll want more of these heartwarming romances, so unless you tell us otherwise, every month we'll send you 4 more wonderful novels to read and enjoy. Always delivered right to your home. And always at a discount off the cover price!

4. Your satisfaction is guaranteed! You may return any shipment of books and cancel at any time. The Free Books and Gifts remain yours to keep!

NO COST! NO RISK!
NO OBLIGATION TO BUY!

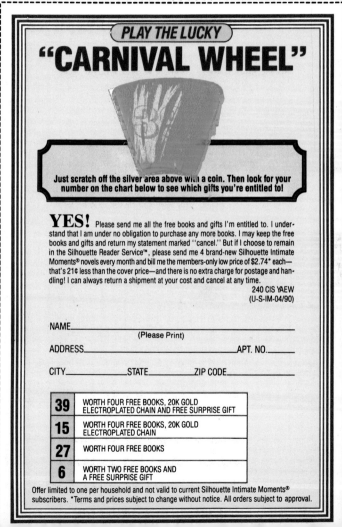

More Good News For Members Only!

When you join the Silhouette Reader Service™, you'll receive 4 heartwarming romance novels each month delivered to your home. You'll also get additional free gifts from time to time as well as our members-only newsletter. It's your privileged look at upcoming books and profiles of our most popular authors!

If offer card is missing, write to: Harlequin Reader Service, 901 Fuhrmann Blvd., P.O. Box 1867, Buffalo, NY 14269-1867

BUSINESS REPLY CARD

First Class   Permit No. 717   Buffalo, NY

Postage will be paid by addressee

SILHOUETTE
READER SERVICE
901 FUHRMANN BLVD
PO BOX 1867
BUFFALO NY 14240-9952

NO POSTAGE
NECESSARY
IF MAILED
IN THE
UNITED STATES

◆ MAIL THIS CARD TODAY! ◆

Ariel nodded, and when she had taken a clean gown from her suitcase she went into the bathroom and closed the door. She stayed in the shower for a long time, letting the water cool her skin and clear her thoughts. She'd been angry with Matt these last few days, but she thought now that perhaps she'd been too sensitive, too defensive about her stepfather. Matt didn't know Emory. He only knew what he'd read in the newspapers or seen on the evening news. Once he met him, he'd feel differently.

When Ariel stepped out of the shower and dried herself, she brushed her long hair and let it hang loose around her shoulders. Then she dabbed a cooling scent on her skin and slipped into a short peach satin gown. She felt a flutter of excitement run through her body, because tonight she intended to make up for the way she'd acted these last few days.

Matt looked at her when she came out of the bathroom, but all he said was, "I won't be long."

She took the spread off the bed and folded it over a chair before she turned back the sheet. Then, her mouth curved in a secret smile, she took the music box out of her suitcase and put it on the nightstand.

The bed was lumpy and the sheets were patched. Instead of two pillows there was one long one. She thought about king-size Hollywood beds with satin sheets and found herself smiling again, because she knew she'd rather be here with Matt than anywhere else in the world with somebody else.

When she heard the shower stop, she lifted the lid off the music box, and with the long pillow behind her head lay down and waited for the door to open.

"That felt good." Matt, a towel wrapped around his waist, stepped into the room. "I hated to get . . ." His voice trailed off. He looked at the music box, then at her. He said, "Ariel?" but didn't move from where he stood.

"This isn't Paris," she said in a tremulous voice. "But we could make it a place we'll never forget."

He took a deep, shaking breath. Then, mobilized into action, he crossed the room and took Ariel into his arms. Relief flooded through him, and he held her, unable to speak until she said, "I'm sorry I've been a grouch, Matt. I—"

He stopped her words with a kiss. "No," he whispered, "don't say anything." He ripped the towel off and pulled her satin-clad body close to his. This was all that mattered now. He wanted to close the world off, to forget about Emory Winston and the bank and the money. There was only Ariel, sweet and warm in his arms. It didn't matter how poor the room, how lumpy the bed, as long as she was with him, this was paradise.

He kissed her eyelids, her nose and her mouth. With gentle hands he caressed her breasts beneath the smooth satin gown, and when she sighed against his lips he whispered her name in an agony of desire.

They made love slowly, tenderly, and when, in that final moment, she cried, "Oh, darling. My darling," he thought his heart would burst with loving her.

Afterward they lay in each other's arms. The white curtains at the windows stirred in a breeze that brought with it the scent of gardenias and night-blooming jasmine.

Matt raised himself on his elbow and looked down at her. "I love you," he said. "I want to spend the rest of my life with you." He kissed her. "Marry me, Ariel. Let's find a *padre* and get married tomorrow."

"Matt, I . . . I don't know what to say."

"Just say you'll marry me." He kissed her, not lightly as he had before, but fiercely, possessively. "Tomorrow," he said against her lips.

Ariel touched the side of his face. "I'll marry you, Matt, but I want to wait until we find Emory, until all of his problems have been taken care of. There's no hurry, is there? Not as long as we know how we feel about each other."

"Ariel, please..." He didn't want to lose her. Tomorrow or the day after that, they might find Emory. And when they did he'd have to issue the warrant he'd brought from L.A. It probably didn't make sense, but in a crazy sort of way he thought that if they were married she'd stick around long enough to give him a chance to explain. Explain what? That he had lied to her? That from the beginning he had used her to find her stepfather?

Matt rolled onto his back, hands above his head, and stared up at the ceiling.

"Don't be upset, darling," Ariel said. "It won't be long. I promise. As soon as all of this is straightened out—"

He reached out, and bringing her up over him, he held her close to his body. "I love you, Ariel," he said against the silken spill of her hair. "No matter what happens, don't ever forget that."

"Nothing's going to happen, Matt. As soon as this is over—"

His kiss stopped her words. He cupped her face between his hands and held her there while his mouth ravaged hers. There was desperation in the kiss, and a hunger that went far beyond a physical need. His body tensed, hardened, and with a low cry he rolled her beneath him.

There was no subtlety now, only the terrible need to hold her and possess her so that she would never be free of him. He took her lips again, then grasped her hips and thrust himself into her. He wanted her to become a part of him, flesh of his flesh, bone of his bone.

Past all barriers of restraint he made her a captive of his passion. And when she held back he tightened his arms around her, plunging harder, deeper.

She cried his name then, and in an eagerness that matched his own she sought his mouth and lifted herself up to meet him thrust for thrust.

"Say it," he demanded. "Tell me! Tell me what I want to hear!"

"I love you," she whispered. "Love you, Matt."

"Never leave me."

"No, never."

"Promise."

"I promise."

"Say it."

"I'll never leave you."

He kissed her again, more gently this time, and whispered against her lips, "I love you, Ariel. Now and for always."

He took her higher and higher to the peak of ecstasy, until finally, in a frenzied voice he cried, "Now, Ariel? Now?"

But she was beyond words, lost in wondrous tingling sensations that shook her to the very depths of her being. All she could do was cling to him while her body soared up and up. She heard him cry, and her arms tightened around him. Brokenly then, she wept his name, "Matt. Oh, Matt."

* * *

Ariel awoke in the first pale light of dawn. She looked at Matt, still asleep beside her, and a feeling of tenderness overwhelmed her. She loved him with an intensity she hadn't ever known she was capable of. Last night he had taken her with a fierceness that had almost frightened her. Then her body had caught fire and she had become as fierce as he, both yielding and demanding, giving and taking, and completely his.

And that, perhaps, was the most frightening of all, the feeling that she had given herself, body and soul, to someone. I love you so much, she wanted to tell him now, and my love makes me vulnerable. So treat me kindly, Matt. Handle all of this love I have to give with care. It's everything that I am, and it's yours, darling, because I love you.

She looked at the music box on the nightstand and smiled, for in a way it was a symbol of their love. "As Time Goes By" had been playing the first time she'd ever seen Matt, that day at the Beverly Hills house when he'd tried to make her feel better with his terrible imitation of Bogie.

Last night they had made love to its music, and she was tempted to let it play now, to awaken Matt to its tinny tune. But his breathing was so even, his sleep so deep, that she hesitated to disturb him. With a smothered sigh she slipped quietly from the bed.

When Ariel came out of the bathroom she stood by the window and looked out at the humid, mist-covered landscape. She wanted a cup of coffee, but the dining room didn't open until seven. She didn't know what to do with herself until then, or until Matt awakened.

She went to the dresser and picked up the photograph that had been taken fifteen years ago. She and her mother and Emory had gone to the place where the photograph had been taken after their work on the dig had been completed, and they'd camped there for the few weeks of their remaining vacation.

Ariel studied the photograph, noting the heavy trees in the background and the scraggly green vegetation. To the left there was a banyan tree, one of the biggest she'd ever seen. She remembered climbing its thick, marvelously twisted trunks and that one day, determined to catch a colorful parrot that had squawked raucously down at her, she'd slipped and fallen.

On the other side of the picture, difficult to see unless you looked very closely, there was a thin stream of water. And she remembered that when you followed its path you came to a waterfall. It had been in this very spot, beside the stream, that Emory had said, "This would be a wonderful place to get lost in, Ariel. If I ever wanted to get away from things this is where I'd come."

She knew she was close to where they had been that long ago summer. Today when Matt awakened they'd explore the area closer to the hotel. Perhaps they could hire an Indian guide, someone who really knew the area.

Still deep in thought Ariel put the photograph back on the dresser, and when she did, she inadvertently brushed Matt's wallet aside and onto the floor.

She turned quickly to make sure that the slight noise hadn't awakened him, then bent and picked the wallet up. It had flipped open and two yellow papers had slipped halfway out onto the floor. She took them out to refold and put back, but when she smoothed one out she saw the words: "LAPD, Warrant for the arrest of..."

Her breath went ragged. The floor tilted and the room spun. She closed her eyes, trying to blot out the words, then forced them open to read: "LAPD, Warrant for the arrest of Emory Winston."

Slowly, her hands shaking so badly she could barely manage, Ariel unfolded the other paper. It was the same, only this time the warrant read: "...for the arrest of Ariel Winston."

She looked at the paper, then at Matt. Sickness rose hot and bitter in her throat, and with a smothered cry she ran into the bathroom.

Five minutes later she came out. Her face was deathly white, but she was calmer now. She did not look at Matt, but dressed quickly in jeans and a T-shirt. She took the photograph off the dresser and put it into her shoulder bag along with a brush and comb and her toothbrush.

Then, without a backward look, she went out and closed the door.

Chapter 10

Matt didn't want to awaken. He was in Casablanca with Ariel, and a five-piece band that sounded exactly like the music box had just started to play "As Time Goes By." Ariel was sitting across the table from him, and she was wearing the same short peach satin gown she'd worn to bed last night. He smiled at her, and she raised a bottle of beer, clinked it against his, and said, "Here's looking at you, kid."

"Of all the gin joints in all the world..." He couldn't remember the rest of the words, so he said, "I love you," instead. He wanted to kiss her, but when he tried to get up out of his chair somebody held him back.

"Let me up," Matt said. "I want to kiss Ariel."

"No," Claude Rains said. "You can't have her because you're a liar and a cheat and we're taking her away." Then Peter Lorre appeared to take Ariel's arm, and in his silky sweet voice said, "Come along, my dear, let me take you away from all this."

"You can't have her!" Matt cried. His heart jumping hard against his ribs, he opened his eyes and reached for her.

She wasn't there. He sat up in bed and looked around the room. It was empty. The bathroom door was open, and he could see that it was empty, too. He glanced at his watch. It was a little after seven.

When he swung his legs over the side of the bed he saw the peach satin gown on the floor. He picked it up and smiled, remembering the moment when he'd taken it from her last night.

He felt strangely uneasy because she wasn't in the room, but he told himself that she'd probably gone downstairs for coffee. Still, a feeling of disquiet that was close to panic made him get up to see if she'd left a note.

There wasn't anything on the bedside table, so he crossed to the dresser. His foot connected with his open wallet and he stopped, puzzled. He picked the wallet up and suddenly his heart began to beat hard in his chest. He looked at the dresser and saw the two warrants, propped side by side against the mirror.

He hung on to the dresser for support and grunted at the pain that ripped through him. "Ariel," he whispered. "Oh my God, Ariel." The pain he knew she must be suffering mingled with his and he gasped aloud.

Last night before he'd gone in to take his shower he'd tossed his wallet up on the dresser along with the car keys, his watch and money. He'd done the same thing every night; Ariel had never evidenced any curiosity about his things. He didn't think she had this morning, either. Probably the wallet had fallen on the floor and she'd picked it up.

He swore at himself for not having gotten rid of the warrants. God knows he wouldn't have used Ariel's, and he doubted, from the things she'd said about Winston, that he'd have had to use a warrant to take him back.

Matt beat a fist on the dresser top. He closed his eyes, knowing how Ariel must have felt when she saw them—when she saw her own name on a warrant for her arrest.

Last night they had made love. He'd asked her to marry him. To her that would have been the cruelest thing of all. He had to find her. He had to explain, to tell her that even though he'd lied to her about who he was and why he'd come to Mexico, he hadn't lied about loving her.

He grabbed his shirt, stepped into his jeans and pulled his boots on, not even aware that he whispered her name, "Ariel," over and over again.

Five minutes later, taking the stairs two at a time, he hurried into the small lobby.

Señor Melendez looked up from his desk. "Ah, *buenos días*, *Señor* McKay. How—"

"Have you seen my wife?"

"*Pues, si*. She went out for a walk almost an hour ago."

"Which way did she go?"

"She took the path through the trees, *Señor* McKay. Just as the other men did."

"What path? Where—?" Matt stared at Melendez. "What other men?"

"The two men who checked in late last night. They came down just a few minutes after *Señora* McKay, and they asked what direction she'd taken."

"And you told them?"

Señor Melendez looked startled. "I saw no reason not to. It is a scenic walk. I thought—"

"What did they look like?"

"Is something wrong, *Señor* McKay?"

"Yes, dammit! What did they look like?"

"The one man was tall and thin. The other..."

Matt raced for the stairs. Upstairs he flung the door of the room open and once inside he slung his suitcase onto the bed and opened it. Throwing his clothes aside he grabbed his gun from a hidden zippered side pocket and shoved it into his belt.

At the door he looked back at the room they had shared. Ariel! Her name screamed in his brain. Then he turned and ran from the room.

Ariel didn't know where she was going, but it didn't matter. She had to get away from the hotel, away from Matt.

Flashes of memory seared in camera-quick images across her brain...the narrow bed in the rustic cabana in Zipolite...the early morning when they swam naked in the sea and the sun turned his skin to tawny gold... moonlight kisses...words whispered in the silence of a darkened room... "I love you, Matt. Love you..."

A strangled cry of anguish escaped her lips. She stumbled and fell and lay for a moment, her face against the humid earth as though seeking comfort from the dampness and the warmth. She began to cry, great gulping ugly gasps that burned her throat. "Fool!" she wept. "Stupid, gullible fool!"

At last she made herself get up. She ran on through the overhang of trees into the denseness of the Mexican jungle. It didn't matter where she went, all she wanted to do was hide from Matt and from the shame of having loved him.

Her side hurt and sweat trickled down between her breasts. But still she ran on, senselessly, blindly, until at last she came to a place where the trees thinned to form an almost pasturelike glen. A stream of water bubbled down the slope of the mountain to form a spring, and when she saw it she went to sit beside it. There, head down on her knees, she rested and tried to think rationally.

But oh, it was hard to face the fact that Matt had lied to her, that from the very beginning he had only used her to get to Emory.

Emory! She had to find him. She had to warn him about Matt.

Matt. Why had he asked her to marry him last night? Because he thought it would be easier to take her back to California—to stand trial for a crime she hadn't committed—if she were legally bound to him?

What if she had said yes? What if today they had gone to find a priest and the priest had married them? How long had Matt planned to go on with the charade of pretending that he loved her?

She raised her head and looked blindly out at the trees. It seemed to her that she could hear his voice echoing in the branches... "Never leave me. Promise me you'll never leave me." And her own words, whispering back, "I promise. I promise."

And all the time he'd had a warrant for her arrest in his wallet.

She lay back on the mossy bank, one arm over her eyes to blot out the sun. She knew that as soon as Matt awoke and found her gone he would come after her, so she made herself get up and bathe her hands and face in the cool spring water.

It was peaceful here with only the bird songs to break the silence. There were orchids of every color, and ferns, bright and green in the sun, which slanted in through the trees. To one side of the clearing there was a giant banyan tree, and through its trunklike branches she could see the bright colors of a macaw. As she watched, it squawked, shattering the silence with its shrill, raucous voice.

I'm going to climb up and pull your tail feathers.

The words were a memory, spoken only in her head, but somehow so real that Ariel looked around as though expecting the child who had spoken them so long ago to be somewhere close by.

Suddenly Ariel's mouth went dry and her heart began to race. She reached in her shoulder bag and pulled out the photograph she'd brought with her from California. She studied it, then the scene around her. And she knew that this was the place where the photograph had been taken.

If this was the place, then Emory had to be somewhere nearby. But where? In which direction?

She ran to the edge of the trees, not sure which way to go. If she could find a path . . . then she saw it, some ten yards from the stream, disappearing into the thick jungle. Excited now, Ariel slung the bag over her shoulder and started up the path. When she entered the trees the jungle grew dark. Twisted vines crisscrossed the ground, and she had to watch her step so she wouldn't fall.

That's what she was doing, watching the ground, when the figure loomed out of the jungle brush in front of her.

Ariel gave a startled cry. She didn't know whether to turn and run or stand her ground. Since she was too afraid to run she stayed where she was.

He was an Indian, short of stature but broad and powerfully built. He had high cheekbones and an eagle nose. His skin was the color of cocoa, and his black hair hung to his shoulders. He had a machete in his right hand.

Ariel took a step back. *"Buen... buenos días,"* she managed to say.

His muscled arm shot straight out, the palm raised, stopping her where she stood. "Go back," he said.

"Why?" She crossed her arms over her chest as though to defend herself. "Is this private land? Does someone own it? Is that why I can't go on?"

"Go back," he said again, and moved toward her.

But Ariel stood her ground. "Look," she said, trying to sound reasonable, "I'm not going to disturb anything. I just want to—"

"It is forbidden. Go back."

Ariel's chin came up. She was a city girl, and if she could brave the wilds of Hollywood Boulevard at night she wasn't going to let one lone Indian keep her from reaching her destination.

She started around him, but he barred her way. She hesitated, forced what she hoped was a reassuring smile, and said, "I was here a long time ago, and I think maybe my father lives somewhere close by. It's terribly important that I find him." She started to reach in her bag, but the Indian grabbed it. That scared her, but it made her mad, too.

"Look at the picture," she said, coming closer to him. "Take it out and look at it."

"Stay," he warned, then he opened her bag and pulled the picture out.

Ariel had no idea how much English he understood, but she pointed to Emory and said, "Father. That's my father."

He looked at the photograph, then at her. Nothing showed on his face when he handed it back to her.

"My name is Chintalpa," he said, and before she realized what he was going to do, he grabbed her wrist and pulled her after him into the brush.

Half an hour went by. Her arms were scratched, and sweat trickled down her face. They were deep into the jungle. The Indian still held her, his left hand clamped around her wrist, while with his other hand he used the machete to hack through the overhang of trees. Once, when he had a particularly hard time breaking through a tangle of vines, Ariel managed to twist away from him. But before she'd taken two steps he grabbed her again.

He swung her around hard and with his face close to hers said, "No! Stay with Chintalpa."

They went on, so deeply into the impenetrable jungle that she knew that if she did manage to escape she'd never find her way out. She was lost in this green and humid heat, being taken God knows where by an Indian as fierce as a character from an old John Wayne movie. He . . .

Suddenly Chintalpa stopped. He listened for a moment.

"What—" Ariel started to say just as he clapped a hand over her mouth and dragged her back into the bushes.

Ariel fought against him, but he held her, one arm across her chest and his hand clamped hard over her mouth. When she heard a rustling sound coming from the trees ahead, she stilled and held her breath, afraid to move.

Someone broke through the underbrush. He stopped for a moment to look behind him, then he turned and she saw that it was Matt.

She tried to cry out, but the Indian's hand clamped harder. "Is he friend or enemy?" he whispered into her ear.

Ariel remained still.

"I take you to your father," he whispered. "Is that man your friend or your enemy?" He eased his hand away from her mouth.

"He..." The words stuck in her throat. She took a deep breath and, closing her eyes, whispered, "He...he is my enemy."

Chintalpa nodded. He held up a warning hand, then, in a crouch, began to move through the trees toward Matt.

Matt stood, unaware of the danger, looking at the ground around him, uncertain which way to go.

Ariel watched him, her hand against her mouth to keep from crying a warning. She told herself that he had betrayed her, and though tears ran down her face she made herself stand silent while the Indian advanced.

In a movement so quick she almost didn't see it, Chintalpa raised his fist and struck Matt a terrible blow behind the neck.

Matt sagged and went down on his hands and knees. Chintalpa grabbed a handful of Matt's hair and lifted his head to strike, but before he could, Matt reached around and grabbed the Indian's legs and pulled him down with him. They rolled on the ground, both of them striking out with their fists. Matt struck Chintalpa in the face, and before he could recover, Matt shot a blow to his ear. Chintalpa grunted, heaved his body away from Matt's and kicked Matt in his side. Matt rolled away, grabbed a handful of earth and threw it at the Indian's eyes.

Ariel, unable to help herself, ran out from her hiding place. Matt turned. He saw her and cried out, "Ariel!

Run! Get away!'' and when he did, Chintalpa smashed a stunning blow to Matt's mouth. Before Matt could recover, he hit him again, and when Matt fought back the Indian grabbed a rock and raised it to strike.

"No!" Ariel screamed.

Chintalpa froze, his arm in midair.

"Don't!" Ariel said brokenly. "No, don't!"

Chintalpa hesitated. "You said he is your enemy."

Matt, flat on his back, the Indian astride him, looked up at her.

In the silence of the jungle a bird began to sing.

"He is my enemy," Ariel said.

"Ariel," Matt said. "Ariel, listen to me."

"Not anymore, Matt."

"I lied about who I was but not about how I feel about you. I—"

Chintalpa cuffed him across the mouth. Holding him with his legs, he reached up and yanked at one of the vines from a nearby tree. He threw Matt over onto his face and tied his hands behind him. Then he tied his feet together, grabbed his ankles and thrust them up behind Matt's back.

When he rolled him onto his back again Ariel saw that Matt's face was bloody. In spite of what he'd done she wanted to run to him. She wanted to cradle his head in her arms and soothe away his pain.

But when Matt said, "You've got to listen to me," she turned her back, fighting hard against the emotions that were tearing her apart. "You lied to me!" she cried. "You used me!"

Chintalpa ripped Matt's shirt off and began rolling it to make a gag.

Matt tried to skitter away, but the Indian hauled him back.

"Ariel, listen to me," Matt cried. "Two men are—"

Chintalpa shoved the gag into Matt's mouth.

"We can't just leave him here," Ariel said.

"I will send somebody back to untie him when we are safely away. Come!"

She looked back at Matt. He looked at her.

Sickness rose in her throat. She took a step toward him. The Indian reached for her, but she shrugged his hand away. "If you'd told me who you were maybe I would have understood," she said brokenly. "I loved you, Matt. I trusted you with my life . . . with my love."

He looked back at her with his bloodied face. His eyes were frantic, and she knew he wanted to say something. But words wouldn't help, not now.

Chintalpa grabbed her arm.

"We go," he said, and turning toward the denseness of trees he pulled her after him.

She looked back at Matt, and a low moan of pain escaped her lips. Then she turned and followed Chintalpa.

Matt lay still. His body hurt from the blows the Indian had inflicted on him, but that pain was as nothing compared to the emotional pain that racked him. For as long as he lived he would never forget the agony on Ariel's face when she turned away.

She had loved him, and he had betrayed that love. It would do no good now to say that he was sorry, that he'd only been doing his job, that he no longer believed she was mixed up in this with her stepfather.

He struggled with his bonds. He had to warn her about the two men who had followed her this morning. In his helplessness and frustration he called himself every kind of a fool for not telling her about the man in Acapulco who'd been watching her. He knew now that the man had followed them from Los Angeles, and that he or an accomplice had followed them from Acapulco. He didn't know if they were after her or her stepfather, he only knew that she was in danger and that he had to help her.

Who in the hell was the Indian? What did he have to do with this? Matt struggled to break free. He cursed his bonds, himself and the Indian. Sweat ran down his forehead into his eyes. He pulled down as hard as he could with his legs and felt the vine that roped his feet and hands together break. Some of the strain eased, and he began to fight against the fastenings that bound his wrists. The wetness of blood oozed down his hands. It made them slippery, and he got one hand free. He yanked the gag out of his mouth, then pulled the vines from his other hand and bent to untie his ankles.

"This way," a voice yelled.

Matt froze. Then he rolled toward the brush, pulling himself along by his hands to get to cover before he was discovered.

"You find the path?"

"Path, hell! Third damn time this morning we've been lost." A man came through the trees. "Over this way," he called as he sank to the ground no more than ten feet from where Matt lay.

He took off the canvas hat he'd been wearing and fanned his face. "What in the damn hell kind of a country is this anyway," he said. "Land of the perpetual sauna. Jeez!"

He was short. He had heavily muscled shoulders and a barrel chest. A fringe of lank greasy hair circled his otherwise bald head, but the hair on his arms and the back of his neck made up for any lack he suffered on his head. His green flowered shirt was soaked with sweat, and he smelled like stale fish.

"Where the hell are ya?" a voice called.

"Over here, dummy. Keep coming."

Matt squinted through the leaves. He saw another man emerge on the other side of the clearing, and sucked in his breath. It was the man from the airport in Acapulco.

"What are you sitting down for?" the skinny guy snapped. "Let's get going."

"This heat is killing me. I gotta rest."

"What you *gotta* do is get off your fat behind." The skinny guy wasn't sweating, but he took a white handkerchief out of the pocket of his button-down shirt and wiped his hands. "Come on, Victor," he said. "Get a move on."

"Move it yourself, Ramon. I gotta rest a minute."

The man called Ramon swore in Spanish. He looked like all the bad guys Matt had ever seen on the old TV shows. His pockmarked face was hollow-cheeked-thin, and his dark eyes were half sunken into his head.

He bent down and examined the ground. "She's got somebody with her," he said.

"McKay?"

"Maybe. Maybe not. Whoever it is he's wearing *guaraches*."

"You think she knows where Winston is?"

"She knows all right."

"You sure he's got the stuff with him?"

"If he hasn't, he'll take us to it."

"Yeah? How ya going to make him do that?"

Ramon smiled. "We get the stepdaughter, and he'll do anything we say."

"And when we get what we're after?"

"We do 'em both."

"I get a crack at the girl before we do," Victor said.

"Of course, *amigo*." Ramon folded his handkerchief and put it back in his pocket.

"What about McKay?"

"He's mine, *compadre*. The crash broke almost every bone in Enrique's body. I promised him before he died that I'd take care of McKay."

The short man stood up. "Okay," he said. "Let's get going." He put the canvas hat back on his bald head. "Maybe if I keep thinking how it'll be when I get the woman alone I won't mind the damn heat so much. I…"

The voices faded away, but Matt didn't move. He lay where he was, so cold now that the sweat had dried on his body.

"I get a crack at the girl," the man called Victor had said. The thought of that short, sweaty, smelly man touching Ariel made the gorge rise in Matt's throat. He gagged, spat, then he sat up and took deep gulping breaths to clear his head.

The Indian had hurt him. So had Ariel. She'd called him her enemy. That hurt, but he didn't blame her, he had it coming. He loved her, but he hadn't trusted her enough to tell her the truth about who he was.

Later, when this was over, he'd make her listen to him. He loved her, she had to believe that. But there wasn't time to think about that now.

Ariel was in danger. The two men, Victor and Ramon, were after her. He had to stop them, any way he could.

Matt reached for the gun he'd stuck in his waistband. It was gone. He'd lost it in the scuffle with the Indian. He swore softly, and on his hands and knees began searching for it. He brushed leaves and fallen branches aside, and when at last he found the the gun he let out the breath he hadn't even known he'd been holding.

He checked the clip and the extra clips in his pocket. He wished now that he'd contacted the police like Brezinski had told him to do, and vowed he would as soon as he could get to a phone.

But right now he had to find the two men who were after Ariel and her stepfather.

And the Indian. Who in the hell was the Indian, and what did he have to do with this?

Chapter 11

Ariel was enclosed in the greenness of jungle, smothered by its terrible damp heat. The thought of Matt, bound hand and foot, helpless against jungle predators, sickened her. For as long as she lived she would never forget the way he had looked at her when she'd turned away from him. But Matt was her enemy, hers and Emory's. She had to think about Emory now.

Chintalpa stopped. Ahead of her, Ariel saw a waterfall.

"We go there," he said.

She followed him through the overhang of trees, only half aware of the beauty around her, of small orchids as colorful as butterflies, moss verbena, bird of paradise and coral vines. He led her close to the waterfall. She wanted to walk into it, to lose herself in the rush of water, to let it wash over her body, wash away all of her thoughts of Matt.

Chintalpa grabbed her wrist again, and for a moment she thought they were going through the waterfall. Instead, he pulled her to one side, behind the rush and the roar of the thunderous cascade.

It was cool in the cavelike recess of rocks. The water was so close she had only to hold out her hand. She felt the cool spray, and when the Indian tried to urge her forward, she shouted, "No, wait," and when he let her go, she reached out and began to splash water over her face and her arms.

Chintalpa stood silently, arms crossed over his chest, watching her. Before, his face had been expressionless, but now the suggestion of a smile crossed his features.

The cold water helped clear Ariel's mind. She closed her eyes and held her face up to the spray, trying to wash away all thoughts of Matt and the way it had been with them last night. But in the rush of water she heard their whispered sighs, their muted words of love. She saw again the smooth clean lines of Matt's hard body, the tapered waist, the narrow hips and the strong legs that had held her captive when she lay beneath him.

Had all the sighs and whispers been a lie? Had the time they'd spent together meant nothing to him? Those were the questions that Ariel knew would torture her for as long as she lived.

"We go now," Chintalpa shouted, and when he put a hand on her arm, she whirled around, still lost in her thoughts of Matt, his name still on her lips.

They passed through the back of the waterfall, out into the heat of the jungle, until at last they came to a small clearing.

"Come," Chintalpa said, gripping her wrist again as though he were afraid she would try to run away.

When they were halfway across the clearing, he stopped. He whistled, waited, then whistled again, before he urged Ariel forward. When they'd gone no more than a dozen or so yards, he pointed, and through the cluster of palm trees at the far end she saw a rustic cottage. The roof was made of palm fronds, the sides were bamboo.

Ariel looked at Chintalpa. Had he brought her here to be his captive? Did Indians do that in Mexico? Dear God, was he going to attack her? To...

An answering whistle sounded through the silence. She looked toward the cabin and a man appeared in the doorway. He shaded his eyes. "Chintalpa?" he called out.

Ariel stopped. Her eyes widened, then with a cry she broke away from the Indian and began to run toward the house.

"Emory!" she screamed. "Emory!"

"I can't believe it's you," he said again and again. "How did you find me? How did you...?" He held her away from him, then hugged her close. "My God, Ariel. What are you doing here? How did you know where I was?" He looked over his shoulder at Chintalpa. "Where did you find her?" he asked.

"In the jungle. She is your daughter?"

Emory smiled down into Ariel's eyes. "Yes," he said with a nod, "she's my daughter."

"A man followed her."

"A man?" Emory held Ariel away from him. "What's he talking about?"

She knew she had to tell Emory about Matt, about how she had trusted him and how he had used her to try to find Emory, about the warrant for his arrest. And hers. But there would be such shame in the telling.

She lowered her eyes. "A man I came to Mexico with," she said.

Emory's brows came together in a puzzled frown. "Where is he now?"

"Back there," Chintalpa said. "Before the waterfall. We fought. I left him there. Later I will send someone to untie him. Someone who will make sure he leaves the area."

Emory's face tensed, and he ran a nervous hand across his face. "Who is he?" he demanded. "Where did he come from and how is it that he came with you? How..." He stopped.

Ariel's face had gone white. She clung to the back of a chair, and he saw her sway. He reached her in one stride and helped her to sit down. "Take it easy," he said gently. "You need something to drink. We can talk when you're feeling better."

"It's the heat," she murmured weakly. "It's so hot."

"I know, sweetheart." He hurried to the kitchen area, where he took three oranges from a bowl of fruit on the wooden counter, squeezed them and brought a tall glass of the juice back to Ariel. "Drink this," he said. "It'll help."

She took the glass gratefully, drank half of it, then leaned back in the chair and closed her eyes. She couldn't believe she had found Emory, and now that she had, there were so many questions she wanted to ask him. Why had he run away? And what about the money? Had he taken it?

Her hands tightened convulsively around the glass. She couldn't bring herself to ask all of the questions that skittered around and around in her head. Not yet.

She opened her eyes and looked around the starkly furnished house. There was a daybed and a chest of drawers against one side of the room. A table, two chairs and a crude wooden stool were next to the kitchen area. The focal point of the room was the easel that stood near the open doorway, and the paintings that leaned against that side of the wall.

"I didn't know you painted," she said.

"It's something I've always had a yen to do. I studied art a long time ago, and for a while I wanted to make a career of it." He smiled. "I wanted to be an archaeologist, too, but somehow I got into the business of making movies."

He went to the open doorway and looked out at the clearing. Ariel had said she'd come to Mexico with a man, and Chintalpa had fought with him. Why? Because he'd known the man was dangerous? That he'd come here to find him?

He knew he would have to leave now, and quickly, but he wanted to give Ariel time to recover from her trek through the jungle and from whatever trauma she'd apparently suffered. When she had, they would leave, but he didn't want to tell her that now.

"When I came here I had time on my hands, and I decided to paint," he said as he turned back to her. "There are a lot of artists living in Oaxaca, so I didn't have any trouble finding supplies. The painting's been a godsend, Ariel. It's helped me keep my sanity these last few months."

She finished the orange juice, and feeling stronger, got up and began to look at the paintings that lined the wall. There was one of the clearing and the jungle beyond. Woven in a tapestry of surrealistic color, the painting was ethereal, almost dreamlike, and yet so real that it seemed to Ariel she could feel the jungle heat and the green dampness closing in on her.

"This is wonderful," she said, then moved on to study the other paintings. There was one of Chintalpa. The Indian looked strong and as primitive as his ancestors must have looked hundreds of years before the Spanish came to Mexico. His skin was the color of sun-baked canvas, and the eyes, staring so boldly out at her, were a fathomless black.

There were other paintings: of a beach at sunset, a forest glade, a group of children. All of the paintings showed more than just a casual talent. They were sensitive and filled with deep emotion and love of both the art and the subject.

She went over to the easel. On it, there was a painting of her mother. "It's...beautiful," she murmured as tears welled in her eyes. "It shows how much you loved her, Emory. How much you miss her." She turned back to him. "You mustn't ever stop painting, not now."

"I don't intend to. If I ever go back..." Emory hesitated. "This is what I want to do with my life now," he finished.

Ariel nodded. "How long have you been here, in this house, I mean?"

"I moved in a couple of weeks after I left Los Angeles. Chintalpa found this place for me." He smiled at the Indian who had taken up a position just inside the door. Arms crossed over his chest, he looked out toward the jungle, watching. He knows there is danger now, Emory thought. He knows we must leave.

"You probably don't remember Chintalpa," Emory said when he turned back to Ariel. "He was just a youngster when we were here with your mother. I've been back in this area a few times since, and I've visited him and his family. I'm very fond of all of them. They're Chontals, and most of them live in a village not too far from here. When the trouble started, I got in touch with Chintalpa.''

Ariel watched her stepfather as he talked. He'd changed in the months since he'd left California. He looked older, and he was thinner than he'd been. But there was a vitality about him, a glow of health that he hadn't had before, especially during those last few weeks before he'd left. His dark hair had a lot of gray, and he had a beard. ''You look like a thin Hemingway,'' she said.

He grinned back at her. ''But I feel more like Gauguin.''

Ariel nodded. ''Yes, I guess you would.'' She hesitated, then she took a deep breath and said, ''Why did you leave, Emory? Why did you go away without telling me?''

He winced, and a look of pain crossed his face. ''At the time I did what I thought was best for you. I wanted to protect you, Ariel, and getting lost seemed the best way to do it.''

''I don't understand. What happened? I know things weren't going well with the picture, but—''

''Not going well?'' His face hardened. ''That's an understatement.'' He took her hand and led her back to the chair, then pulled up the stool and sat beside here. ''I'd wanted to make *Winter Love* for a long time, Ariel. I knew it was going to be an expensive picture to make and that backing would be hard to come by. But I wanted it so damn bad that I was willing to do almost anything. Continental Trust had loaned me twenty-five million dollars, with the house and the furnishings as collateral, and—''

"They took the house," she said. "They took every-thing."

Emory's face went white. "I...I didn't think they would do it that soon. I thought I had time, that I could somehow manage to pay off the loan." He reached for Ariel's hand. "You had to sell it all?"

"Yes, Emory. The Miró and the Chagall, the arti-facts."

"Oh, my God." He put his head in his hands and moaned. "And you were the one who had to do it, who had to stand by and watch everything go." He raised his face, tortured with all that he was feeling, and looked at her. "Were you able to save anything?"

Ariel shook her head. "It's gone, Emory. All of it."

He got up and began to pace the room. His face had drained of color and his hands had curled into fists. "Damn them," he muttered. "Damn them to hell!"

"What? Who are you talking about?"

"I should have known better. I would have if I hadn't been so determined to make the picture." He hit his fist against his open palm. "I should have known it was too easy. I shouldn't have trusted them."

Ariel got up and went to him. "Emory, please. I don't know what you're talking about. You're not making any sense." She took his hands and led him over to the chair, then sat on the stool in front of him. "Tell me what happened," she said.

He swallowed hard. "The money from the bank wasn't enough. I'd already spent over half of it and we were way over budget. I started putting feelers out, trying to find some big money. I'd just about given up when a group of men from Chicago approached me. A couple of them came out to the coast. They said they wanted to get in-volved with the movie business. It happens every day, moneyed men who think they can make a killing if the picture goes over big, men who like the idea of rubbing elbows with the Hollywood crowd.''

Emory ran a hand through his hair. "At first, it was all right. The money came in when I asked for it. Then they started coming onto the lot. They wanted a change of leading men, and when I balked, they said they'd back out. I told them I wanted a few days to think about it. The next day there was an accident on the set."

"I remember! A light fell. It almost hit Laura."

Emory nodded, his face grim. "That night I got a call from the man who'd made the first contact, a man named George Trevino. He mentioned the accident. Wasn't it a shame, he said. And wouldn't it be too bad if there were another accident and someone was seriously injured, one of my principals or..." He stopped, unable to go on.

"Or you?"

He shook his head. "No, Ariel, not me. He threatened you."

Her gray eyes widened in disbelief.

"So I changed the leading men." Emory got up and began to pace.

"Why didn't you tell me what was happening?"

"Because these weren't ordinary hoods, Ariel. They were big-time bad medicine. I did some checking. Trevino and his men weren't who I'd thought they were. They were involved with a Colombian drug cartel, Ariel. It was drug money they invested in *Winter Love*. That's why they invested, to launder their dirty drug money."

Her face went as white as his had been, and it was a moment or two before she could speak. "What . . . what happened when you found out?"

"I told Trevino I wanted out. He told me I couldn't back out, that I was in on it now. I threatened to go to the FBI, and he..." A muscle jumped in Emory's cheek, and his fists tightened again.

"He what?" Ariel asked.

"He threatened you again. This time he was pretty specific about what would happen."

She stared at him. "You should have gone to the FBI, anyway. We could have asked for protection."

"I couldn't take a chance, not with your life." Emory took a deep breath. "So I took their money and I ran."

"You took the money?" Ariel shook her head, unable to believe what he'd said. "You actually took the money?"

"*Their* money." He saw the expression on her face, and pain twisted through him. "I converted everything into diamonds. They're in a safe-deposit box in a bank in Mexico City along with the film. I haven't touched the diamonds and I don't intend to."

"But why?" She felt as though her world had turned upside down. "Why did you take it? I don't understand."

"I took it, and I wanted them to know that I had, so that Trevino and his boys would come after me. So they'd leave you alone. And that's what they did, Ariel. They're looking for me now, not you. They've taken a contract out on me."

"A contract?" Her mouth went cotton-dry. "You mean they've hired somebody to..." She couldn't go on.

Emory nodded. "I've got a friend in L.A. who I've been in touch with a couple of times since I've been here. He's got connections in Chicago. It's true. They've hired a hit man, and they're paying him a hundred thousand dollars to do the job."

She couldn't take it in. Things like this didn't happen in real life, they only happened in detective novels or foreign intrigue films. Not to Emory or to her.

"All these weeks I've been away I've wondered if they might try to get to me through you," he said. "I wanted to warn you, but I was sure the phone had been tapped, either by Trevino's people or by the police. I couldn't take the chance." He didn't want to go on but he knew he had to. She had to know.

"That's been my biggest worry," he said gently. "That they'd arrange to have one of their men get close enough so that you'd trust him and maybe lead him here. It could have been anybody, Ariel, even somebody pretending to be a cop. A man will do a lot of things for a hundred thousand dollars. He..."

But Ariel had stopped listening. The voice in her head had drowned out the rest of Emory's words. A hit man. The words seared through her brain.

My God! Oh, my God! Matt! All along it had been Matt. Matt who had told her he loved her. Matt who had asked her to marry him.

The room closed in on her. She must have said something, must have uttered a cry. Chintalpa swung away from the door. Emory reached out a hand to steady her.

He said, "Ariel? What is it, Ariel?"

She turned her stricken face to his. "He's here," she gasped. "He came to the auction. He said he was a security man. He..." Sweat beaded on her forehead. "I asked him to come to Mexico with me." She touched Emory's face. "What have I done?" she whispered. "Oh, Emory, what have I done?"

"I should have killed him." Chintalpa turned away from the door. "I will go back. I—"

"No." Emory held up his hand to stop the Indian. Ignoring Ariel for a moment, he said, "We've got to leave."

Chintalpa nodded. "We will go to my village. After I have taken care of the man who looks for you, we will find another place."

"I'm...I'm so sorry," Ariel's voice broke. "I only wanted to find you, to help you. Instead I've ruined everything."

She tried to think, to gather her thoughts so that she could tell Emory what he needed to know. "I met him at the house, when the bank had the auction. I thought he was a security man. This morning he was still sleeping when I woke up and—"

Emory swung around, his face tight with anger. "You were lovers?"

She was trembling so much now that she could barely get the words out. "Yes," she whispered. "We...we were lovers."

"The bastard!"

"That doesn't matter now."

She'd gone hollow inside. Her world had come crashing down, and she knew that she could never be the same again. But she would think about that later. Think about Matt later.

"He was asleep," she said again. "I got up and somehow I knocked his wallet off the dresser. When I picked it up I saw the warrants."

"Warrants?"

"For your arrest."

"You said 'warrants.'"

"One for you and one for me." Ariel made herself go on. "They looked real, Emory. Maybe he really is a policeman." She could have borne that. She could have told herself that Matt had only been doing his job, that what he'd done was despicable but perhaps understandable.

Emory shook his head. "We've got to get out of here," he said to Chintalpa. "Help me get my gear together."

"When you are safe I will go back and kill him," the Indian said.

"No!" The cry tore from Ariel's throat.

Emory looked at her. "You were in love with him, weren't you?"

"Yes, I . . . I was in love with him."

Emory swore under his breath. "Someday, when this is over, I'm going to find him. And when I do..." He was so filled with anger that he couldn't go on. "What's his name? Tell me his name."

"It's Matt," she whispered. "Matt McKay."

"McKay?" Emory frowned. "I know that name from somewhere. I—"

Chintalpa stepped back from the doorway. "Someone comes," he whispered.

Emory froze. He looked at Ariel. "He's found us," he said. "Oh, my God, he's here."

Chapter 12

Matt plucked a scrap of Ariel's shirt off a thorny bush. He wasn't much of a tracker, but this was the second piece of cloth he'd seen.

Sweat dripped down into Matt's eyes. His head ached and his wrists were cut from having wrestled with his bonds. And the heat! He'd never experienced this kind of heat, not even in the desert. It was dry in the desert, but here it was as though he'd been enveloped by steam. It rose from the jungle floor and burned down from the sun. If he got out of this alive he'd give serious thought about moving to Alaska.

He saw another piece of material hanging from a bush. It was green, a piece of the flowered shirt worn by the man called Victor.

Matt quickened his pace. He had to find her before they did.

When he heard the waterfall he hurried toward the sound, and ran forward when he saw it, wondering how he could get around it. There wasn't a path. He either had to go forward, into the waterfall, or go back. And dammit all, he wasn't going back. There had to be a way around the cascade of water.

It took Matt almost ten minutes to find the way behind the waterfall. Once he did, he stopped to wash the blood off his wrists and let the water splash over his head. He cupped his hands and drank, then turned and ran on.

Ariel, he thought. I'm coming Ariel. Hang on, my love.

Chintalpa eased close to the door.

A shot rang out, whumped hard into his body and slammed him against the doorjamb. He slumped to the floor. More shots rang out. Emory rushed forward and pulled Chintalpa back into the house.

"There's a rifle in the chest," he yelled to Ariel. "Get it!"

For a moment she was too frozen to move. Then she whirled and ran to the chest.

"Keep down," Emory ordered.

She threw the chest open. The rifle lay on top of some clothes, next to a box of bullets. She grabbed the rifle and the bullets and ran back to Emory.

"There's a revolver, too. Find it and load it."

Without a word Ariel turned. Behind her she heard the bark of the rifle. She dropped to the floor and crawled back to the chest. The revolver wasn't on top as the rifle had been. Frantically she threw clothes and books aside. Her hand touched metal, then a box of bullets. She grabbed them and pulled them out. With her back against the chest she loaded the gun, thankful that years ago Emory had shown her how to do it, as well as how to use a gun.

Use it! On Matt? Ariel stifled a moan, then scurried across the floor to Emory.

"Give me the gun." He thrust the rifle at her. "Load it, then see what you can do for Chintalpa."

She loaded the rifle. A bullet whizzed in through the door and hit the chest.

"Keep down!" Emory cried.

She flattened herself against the floor and crawled to Chintalpa. He lay facedown, sprawled with his arms above his head. She took him by one shoulder and the side of his waist and tried to turn him over. He was a big man, and though there wasn't an ounce of fat on him, he was heavy with muscle. She managed to get him onto his back and gasped when she saw the pool of blood on the floor.

His eyes fluttered open and he groaned.

"Lie still, Chintalpa," she said.

The wound was in the fleshy part of his shoulder. She started to rip off the bottom part of her T-shirt when Emory said, "Load!" and skidded the revolver across the floor.

Ariel loaded it and slid it back to him, then bent over the Indian. She tore at the bottom half of her T-shirt, ripped a strip off and began to bind Chintalpa's shoulder.

"How is he?" Emory called out.

"It's a shoulder wound."

"One of them is trying to circle around to the side. You'll have to shoot."

"One of them?" Ariel whirled around and stared at Emory. "But Matt was alone. He—"

"Hurry!" He shoved the rifle at her. "Shoot while I load."

Ariel took his place at the window. Her heart was beating hard now, not so much from fear as from a strange kind of hope that maybe it wasn't Matt who was shooting at them. Emory had said "they." He'd said "one of them." Matt didn't have anybody working with him.

She remembered the man in the blue car who'd been after them on the road from Puerto Angel to Oaxaca. Matt's fear had been real that day. If it had been an accomplice in the blue car, someone he knew, he wouldn't have reacted the way he had.

A figure darted out from around the side of the house. She fired, missed and fired again. The man whirled and she got a look at him. It wasn't Matt.

Emory crawled over toward the half-open door. He fired, then ducked back. He glanced at Chintalpa. "How are you doing, *amigo*?" he asked.

"Do not worry about me." The Indian dragged himself up to a sitting position. "Give me the rifle, Winston. Take your daughter. Get the jeep."

"Jeep?" Ariel said. "You've got a Jeep?"

"Out in the back, hidden in the bushes." Emory looked down at the Indian. "Do you think you can walk?"

Chintalpa tried to get up, but his legs wouldn't support him. "I cannot walk," he said. "But I can shoot. Go, Winston. I can hold them off until you get away."

"No way, José." Emory summoned a grin. "You and I are in this together." He reached in his trouser pocket and took out a key. "Here," he said to Ariel, and tossed the key to her. "When I tell you to run, you run. Keep low. Go to your right out the door. Circle around back then go left for about ten yards. You'll see the Jeep. Take it and get the hell out of here."

Ariel stared at him in disbelief. "And leave you and
Chintalpa here?" She shook her head and, imitating him,
said, "No way, José."

"Dammit, Ariel, this is no time to argue. You'll do as
I say or—"

A barrage of bullets stopped him.

"If you are going, it must be soon," Chintalpa said. "I
do not think we can hold them much longer."

Emory looked at Ariel. "Please," he begged. "Do
what I've told you."

But she shook her head. "I won't leave you," she said.

Matt heard the gunfire. He stopped, then ran forward
through the bushes. He kept running, but stopped when
he came to the edge of the clearing and saw the house. If
he wanted to reach it he had to cross the open field. If he
did, one of them might see him.

Eyes narrowed against the sun, his lean face hard, Matt
looked around. He'd have to go into the jungle again and
circle in back of the house. It would take longer, but if
Winston could hold out another five or ten minutes he
could take the two men from the rear.

He slipped into the jungle and ran in the direction of
the shots. He heard only sporadic gunfire coming from
the house. "Keep shooting, Winston," he said under his
breath.

Five minutes later he was around the house, but too far
back. He had to get closer. He had to... He saw something partially hidden by the trees. He stopped, not sure
what it was, then slowly crept forward. With a start he
said, "I'll be damned, it's a Jeep."

Matt grinned. Then the grin died. He listened. The
gunfire had stopped. So, for a moment, had his heart. He
looked toward the house.

"No!" he cried. "Oh my God, no!"

The roof was on fire!

Frantically he tore at the shrubs that half covered the machine, and when he had thrust them aside he climbed into the Jeep and reached under the dashboard. "Come on," he muttered as he fumbled for the wires. "Come on, dammit. You did this when you were a kid. You know how. Do it!"

The engine caught. He backed, then straightened and started forward.

"I'm coming," he said under his breath. "I'm coming, Ariel."

It had been the fat man who'd sprinted up from the side. Ariel had been watching. She saw him pull back his arm, heave, and suddenly what looked like a fireball sailed through the air and thudded up onto the roof.

"Emory!" she screamed.

He turned, alarm in his eyes. "What? What is it?"

"One of them threw something...a torch...up onto the roof. He—"

"What!" He could hear the crackle of the flames. They had to get out...fast! In another two minutes the roof would be ablaze and the walls would catch.

Chintalpa, with his back to a wall, pushed himself up. "Run!" he shouted at Emory. "I'll hold them off."

Emory looked at his friend, then at Ariel. She waited for him to tell her what to do.

Emory knew that the minute they stepped out of the door the two men would have them. They might not shoot him because he could tell them where the money was. But they wouldn't care about Chintalpa or Ariel.

He raised the rifle. Without turning to look at Ariel, he said, "The diamonds are in the Bancomer in Colonia

Juarez, near Insurgentes." He slid his wallet across the floor. "The key for the safety deposit box is in the wallet."

Flames licked down the walls from the roof.

"I'm not going to leave you," she said.

"There isn't time to argue. Chintalpa and I will cover you. Get the Jeep. You'll find a dirt road half a mile from here." He fired another round of bullets. "Take it until you see a stand of pines off to your right. Turn off the road there. It'll take you to the Chontal village. Tell the people that you're my daughter. They'll take care of you."

The roof and one wall were in flames. The other walls smoldered. In another two or three minutes the whole house would go.

"They won't kill me," Emory cried, desperate to get her out of the house before it collapsed. "I can lead them to the diamonds."

She felt the terrible heat of the fire.

"Go!" Emory grabbed her arm and gave her a shove. "Dammit, Ariel," he shouted above the roar of the fire. "Get the hell out of here before—"

A rapid burst of gunfire stopped his words. One of the men who'd been shooting at them yelped in pain. Emory swung around. Where had the shot come from? What—?

The Jeep tore around the side of the burning house and screeched to a halt in front of the door.

"Come on!" Matt yelled.

"Who...?" Emory grabbed Ariel's arm. "Go on," he yelled. "I'll get Chintalpa."

Her eyes were wide with shock. Matt! How had he...?

Blazing palm fronds crashed in back of her. She ran for the door, hesitated, then grabbed the painting of her mother off the easel and snatched up her shoulder bag.

"Go on!" Emory cried.

She sprinted for the Jeep. Matt lay over the front seat, firing in the direction of the bushes at the side of the house. She flung herself into the back.

The house was an inferno. Another part of the roof crashed in. She screamed for Emory. He came out, half carrying, half dragging Chintalpa.

"Get him in the back," Matt yelled.

Ariel laid the painting on the floor and reached out to help her stepfather get Chintalpa in next to her. Matt swung back into the driver's seat as Emory got in beside him. He gunned the motor and the Jeep leapt forward. Emory grabbed the rifle from Chintalpa and fired a round of shots.

"Straight ahead," he told Matt. "There's a dirt road." He turned back to Ariel. "Stay down. Keep Chintalpa down."

A bullet whizzed over her head. She didn't need any urging. She ducked down, pulling the Indian down with her, shielding his body with hers.

"Only a little farther," Emory said when they were out of range. "Just ahead. We stay on the road for half a mile." He looked at Matt. "Who in the hell are you?" he asked.

"Name's McKay." He glanced quickly over his shoulder to make sure that Ariel was okay. "I tried to tell her this morning that somebody was following her but Hiawatha clobbered me. There were two of them. They came along a little while after Ariel and your pal had left. I managed to roll myself into the bushes so they wouldn't see me. They—'' Matt saw the road ahead and turned into it. "Where do we go from here?" he asked.

"I'll tell you when we get there. There's a path off to your right. It's rough but we can manage it with the Jeep."

"They'll be after us just as soon as they have transportation. Have you got a place to hide?"

"The Chontal village." Emory pointed to the stand of pines just ahead of them. "There," he said, pointing. "That's where we'll turn."

Matt slowed down. The path was so well hidden from the road that he almost didn't see it. Rutted and rough, it was barely wide enough for the Jeep. He stopped talking and paid attention to where he was going.

Ariel, almost in a state of shock from the fire and Matt's sudden appearance, hadn't spoken since she'd jumped into the vehicle. She stared at the back of Matt's head, wondering where he'd come from, how he'd gotten loose from his bonds. She looked at Chintalpa. He too was staring, surprised by Matt's sudden appearance. Then he slumped against her and she saw that the bleeding had soaked through the makeshift bandage.

The Jeep hit a rut. Chintalpa muttered in pain and blood seeped out of the wound.

"Give me your shirt," she said to Emory.

He turned around, then ripped his shirt off. "Can you manage?" he asked.

"Yes." Ariel tried to steady herself against the bouncing. "But you've got to stop for a minute."

Matt slowed the Jeep, then stopped and left it idling.

Ariel tore at the cotton with her teeth, then ripped Emory's shirt into strips.

Matt swung around in his seat. "Let me help," he said.

Ariel, without looking up, handed him a strip of the white cloth. "Make a pressure pack," she said.

Matt nodded, and when it was ready he leaned over the seat and pressed it against the Indian's wound.

Chintalpa opened his eyes and stared at Matt. "You fight pretty good, *gringo*," he muttered.

"You're not bad yourself." Carefully Matt eased Chintalpa up to a sitting position and held him there while Ariel wrapped the bandage around his shoulder.

"Are you all right?" he asked her.

Ariel looked at him, then quickly away. "I'm all right," she said.

Matt took a deep breath. "You'll have to try to hold him steady when we start again. This is going to be hard on him." He turned to Emory. "How far do we go on this?"

"Six miles."

"Your friend's badly hurt. I hope he can make it."

"He'll make it."

"Do they have a doctor where we're going?"

Emory shook his head. "Only a *curandero*, a medicine man."

"I hope he knows how to dig a bullet out."

"I doubt that he does. But once it's out he'll know how to cure the wound." Emory glanced back at Chintalpa. Ariel had her arms around the Indian and was doing her best to cushion him against the rutted path.

It took them almost thirty minutes to go the six miles, and Matt breathed a sigh of relief when he finally saw the scattering of huts among the palm trees. They were simple and rustic, smaller than the house where Emory had lived. In place of doors most of the houses had beaded curtains or a piece of cloth hanging in the doorway. There were braziers for cooking in front of some of the houses, and hammocks hung between many of the trees. Beyond them, Ariel could see the blue waters of the Gulf of Tehuantepec.

As soon as the Jeep entered the village curious children ran out of the huts. A few adults followed, and a man called out, "Winston? Is it you?"

"Yes, Tlalixa," Emory said when Matt stopped. "Chintalpa has been shot. Where is the *curandero*?"

The man he had called Tlalixa stepped up to the Jeep. He looked at Chintalpa, gasped, then pointed to a hut set far back among the palm trees. "Achiutla lives there," he said in Spanish. "I will go with you. He speaks only Chontal."

He ran ahead to show the way, and when Matt had parked in front of the cabin, Tlalixa called out, "Achiutla!" and said something else in a language Matt didn't understand.

A thin old man stepped out of the doorway. Tlalixa pointed to the Jeep, and the old man hobbled over. He peered in, then motioned for Tlalixa to bring the wounded man inside his hut.

Chintalpa, barely conscious now, sagged between Matt and Tlalixa when they carried him into the hut. Achiutla indicated the straw mat in the corner of the semidark room. They laid him there.

Emory and Ariel had followed them to the door. Ariel peered inside and sucked in her breath. The straw mat lay on a dirt floor. There was a wooden stool covered with animal skin in one corner of the room, a few cracked dishes and a table that held jars of herbs, some clay pots and a pestle.

Achiutla leaned over Chintalpa and began to unwrap the bandage. He tossed it aside and began to poke around the edge of the wound with dirty fingers.

"Don't do that!" Ariel stepped into the small room before Emory could stop her. "Tell him," she said to Emory. "Tell him not to do that."

Emory put a restraining hand on her arm. "He's the only doctor these people have ever had, Ariel. We're outsiders. We can't interfere."

"But his hands are dirty," she protested. "If he touches the open wound he'll infect it."

"Do you know anything about taking out a bullet?"

Ariel shook her head. "I took a first aid course, but it didn't cover bullet holes."

"I can do it," Matt said.

Emory raised a questioning eyebrow. "Where'd you learn?"

"The army."

"Okay. Let me see what I can do." Emory knelt down beside Chintalpa. "The bullet has to come out," he said. "It's not that I lack faith in your *curandero*, for I know he has many skills. But I don't think he's knowledgeable about bullet wounds. *Señor* McKay is. Will you allow him to remove the bullet and clean the wound? After he has, the *curandero* will use his medicine to take the poison out."

Chintalpa looked from Emory to Matt. "You can do this?" he asked.

"I have done it before."

Chintalpa studied Matt with narrowed eyes, alert now in spite of his wound and the loss of blood. "We fought. I hurt you and left you in the jungle. Now is your chance to take revenge."

"Do you think I am that kind of man?" Matt asked quietly.

The Indian stared at him for a long moment. "No," he said at last. "I do not think so." He raised himself on his good arm and spoke quickly to Tlalixa, then to the *curandero*.

Tlalixa nodded. The old man grumbled, but he gave a nod of assent.

"I'll need a knife," Matt told Emory. "And anything else you can find you think we might need: alcohol, a pot of water, soap, clean bandages."

"I'll see to it."

Matt turned to Ariel. "I'll need some help. Can you handle it?"

She nodded. "What do you want me to do?"

"Sterilize the knife and whatever else your stepfather can find. And I'll need you to help hold the wound open while I probe." To Emory, Matt said, "Let's get him outside. It's too dark in here. I won't be able to see." He scowled down at the dirty mat. "Try to find a couple of clean sheets, too, one to cover the mat and one to put over him."

Together, lifting the mat under Chintalpa, they carried him outside into the sun. Tlalixa built a fire in the brazier and put a pot of water on to boil. Emory went for the things Matt had asked for, and when he returned and the knives had been boiled, Matt knelt beside the Indian. He cleaned the wound with soap and water, then said, "This is going to hurt like hell."

"Do not hurt me too much, *gringo*, or when I am well I will show you the way a Chontal can fight when he's really mad."

"I'll be ready for another go-round whenever you are," Matt answered, not altogether joking. He glanced up at Ariel. "Give me the knife," he said. "Then hold his arm steady."

She'd never done anything like this before. The wound was raw and sore. Chintalpa had lost a lot of blood. She knew that trying to take the bullet out without any kind of an anesthetic was going to be painful, especially with the "instruments" they had—a small paring knife and a longer, thinner knife. Any self-respecting surgeon would have thrown his hands up in horror.

Matt picked up the long, thin knife. "Here we go, pal," he said, and made an incision.

Chintalpa grunted but he didn't move.

Blood ran from the wound, and Ariel wiped it away.

"Stretch the wound open while I probe," Matt said. "That's it." And to Chintalpa, he said, "Don't move, *amigo*."

"He's fainted," Ariel whispered.

"Good. That makes it easier for all three of us."

In less than fifteen minutes Matt had found the bullet, taken it out, cleaned the wound, and with Ariel's help had bandaged the Indian's shoulder. When Chintalpa regained consciousness, Matt said, "I wish I had something to give you for the pain."

"I will drink some mescal. That will help." Chintalpa offered his good hand. "Thank you," he said. "Later we will speak."

Matt stood up. "Yes, later." He turned away from the Indian and to Ariel he said, "Right now, you and I have to talk."

"There isn't anything to talk about." She turned and walked away from him.

He didn't blame her, but sooner or later they had to have it out. She had to believe that even though he'd lied about who he was, he hadn't lied about loving her.

It hurt him to look at her, because her face was so drawn and pale. What was left of the T-shirt was torn and caked with dirt. Her face and her arms were scratched.

He wanted to soothe the cuts and bruises, and ease the pain that he had caused.

Give it time, he told himself. Ariel has been through a lot. She's hurt and angry, but she loves you. She said she did. But he wondered as he watched her move closer to Emory if she would ever be able to forgive him.

Tlalixa gave them an empty hut and three clean mats.

"Stay here as long as you want to," he told Emory. Then asked, "Do you think the men who did this to Chintalpa know where you are?"

"Not yet." Emory ran a hand over his beard. "But if they know that Chintalpa is a Chontal they might come to the village."

"How many were they?"

"Two, but I think McKay got one of them." Emory hesitated. "You and your people have been good to me, Tlalixa. Chintalpa is like the son I never had. The men who are after me have no scruples. I don't want to bring harm to your village or your people."

Tlalixa shook his heed. "You are our friend, Winston. Your enemies are our enemies. Our home is your home."

"*Gracias, amigo.* Nevertheless, we will leave as soon as we can."

And then? Emory wondered. Matt McKay wasn't the hit man that Trevino had hired to kill him, but he'd come to Mexico with a warrant for his arrest. Emory knew that his days of seclusion were over. He'd have to go back now, he had no choice.

Chapter 13

In the early evening, when the heat of the day had cooled, Ariel went down to the water to bathe. The Gulf was far enough away from the village so that no one would see her, and she desperately needed this time alone.

Too much had happened. Matt had betrayed her, then he had rescued her. She hadn't had time to sort out all of the things she was feeling.

It seemed incredible that less than twenty-four hours ago she had been happier than she'd ever been in her life. Matt had asked her to marry him. "We'll find a *padre*," he'd said. "We'll get married tomorrow."

Tomorrow. Today.

Her whole world had turned upside down. The man in whose arms she had lain only a few hours before had only been using her. His whispered words of love had all been make-believe.

With an anguished cry, Ariel pulled off her jeans. Clad in her panties and the torn T-shirt, she ran into the water, dived headlong into a wave, and began swimming as fast as she could, trying to drive all thoughts of Matt from her mind.

When she stopped to rest she lifted her face to the last rays of the sun. Blinded by the glare, adrift in the silent water, it seemed to Ariel that she could see in the shifting clouds the pieces of the time she had spent with Matt. Like the broken shards of a kaleidoscope, they danced before her eyes . . . the first time they'd made love . . . his magnificent nakedness . . . his hands touching her in ways that had made her plead for him to take her.

The quiet splash of the waves became their whispered sighs and words of love. The gentle caress of the water against her breasts became the touch of his hands. Her breasts began to throb, and a familiar longing ache made her whimper in need. Her tears mingled with the sea because she wanted him just as much as she had that day in Zipolite.

The sun settled into the golden sea, and she looked back toward the shore where lantern light flickered like fireflies through the gathering darkness. Then she turned away and swam until she was exhausted, until the terrible ache had lessened.

When she rolled onto her back she looked up at the first night stars and the thin slice of the new moon. Unable to bear the beauty of the night, she closed her eyes and floated, arms outstretched in the cool dark water.

Finally, so tired she could barely move her arms and legs, Ariel began to swim toward the shore.

Matt watched her come up out of the water. Barefoot and bare-chested, he waited under one of the palm trees. By the light of the new moon he could see that she was wearing only white bikini panties and the tattered shirt. Her long blond hair streamed down her back, and when she reached the shoreline she stopped and stood, motionless, looking up at the stars.

She was so beautiful. Tears stung his eyes because he loved her, because he was afraid he had lost her.

He stepped out of the shadow of the palm. "Ariel?" he said softly.

She turned, trying to see him through the darkness.

"You shouldn't swim alone," he said. He remembered the undertow that had almost taken her away from him in Zipolite, and that after he had pulled her from the sea they had made love for the first time. Jagged pain cut through Matt's body. No one had ever made him feel what he'd felt with Ariel that day. He'd known then that she was the only woman he'd ever want for as long as he lived.

He couldn't lose her now.

"We have to talk," he said as he went to her. "About us."

She looked at him, her face shadowed by moonlight. "Us?" she said in a tight little voice. "There isn't any us, not anymore, Matt."

"Ariel, please." He moved as though to touch her, but she backed away from him.

"You lied to me," she said.

The pain in her voice ripped through him.

"You're not a security man, you're a policeman."

"No." Matt shook his head. "I work for Continental Trust."

A look of surprise flickered across her face, then her lips curved in a bitter smile. "So that's why you were at the auction, you had a vested interest in everything that was sold. I'm sorry about the music box. It probably wouldn't have brought more than twenty-five dollars, but I'll give you a check for it just as soon as we're back in L.A."

She took a step toward him, chin raised in defiance, her eyes flashing her anger. "But the money from the auction wasn't enough, was it, Matt? You had to take me, too." Her throat worked as she tried to swallow her rage and her tears. "Was I any good, Matt? How much did you take off of what Emory owes for each time we made love?"

"Ariel! For God's sake!" Matt gripped her upper arms and pulled her against him. "Don't demean what we have."

"What we have?" She tried to laugh. "We don't have anything, Matt. We never did. You used me to get to Emory." Her voice broke. "You used me."

"No!" He pulled her into his arms. She fought against him, but he wouldn't let her go. He had to explain, had to tell her... But the feel of her breasts under the tight, wet T-shirt drove all of his words away. He moved against her, lost in the feel of her taut breasts against his bare chest. When she tried to get away he put his hand against the small of her back and pressed her close against his arousal.

Ariel cried out and tried to push him away, but he grasped both of her wrists and pulled her closer. She tried to twist away from him then, and the feel of her body, cool and wet against his, set him on fire. He put one hand behind her head. Tightening his fingers against her scalp he forced her face to his and kissed her.

"Listen to me," he said against her lips. "I love you. I—"

She pulled a hand free and tried to shove him away, crying in anger and frustration. "I hate you," she wept. "Hate you—"

He found her mouth and kissed her again, hard, then gripped her firm little bottom and shoved the bikini panties down so he could cup the cool twin fullnesses. He had to take her now, he'd go crazy if he didn't. He could pull her down onto the warm sand and strip her wet panties off. He could . . .

Suddenly Ariel's lips softened under his and she began to answer his kiss with a hunger that matched his own.

He gasped with pleasure, and his body grew taut with need. He found her breasts, and the small peaks hardened against his fingertips.

"No," she whispered. "No, no, no!" She began to cry then, soft wretched sobs, shaking her head as though to deny all that she was feeling. Before he could stop her, she turned and ran across the sand to the village.

Matt started after her, then he stopped. Hands clenched at his sides he looked up at the stars. "Ariel," he whispered. "Oh, Ariel."

Emory waited until Ariel had fallen asleep before he said, "I'd like to see you outside, McKay."

Matt glanced over at Ariel. She'd pulled one of the mats over to a corner of the hut and lay with her back to the open door. That's where she'd been when he finally came back from the beach. And Emory had told him she'd been exhausted from her swim and had gone to sleep almost as soon as she'd returned.

Matt followed Emory outside. To delay all of the things that had to be talked about, and because he really wanted to know how Chintalpa was, he said, "Mind if we check on Chintalpa first?"

"I saw him while you were down at the beach. Achiutla had given him some kind of a sleeping potion, so I didn't wake him. He didn't have a fever though, and his pulse rate seemed normal. I think he's going to be okay." Emory leaned back against one of the palms. "He wouldn't have been okay if you hadn't taken the bullet out. You did a good job. Thanks."

"It's been a long time since I had to do anything like that."

Emory reached in his pants pocket and pulled out a crumpled pack of cigarettes. After he'd lit one, he said, "Who are you, McKay? I've heard your name, but I don't remember where or in what context. I don't know many cops."

"I'm not a cop. I'm a VP of Continental Trust. Every once in a while, when a lot of money is involved, I act as a troubleshooter."

"How'd you get the warrants?"

"A lieutenant from the LAPD had them issued to me." Matt's voice hardened. "What did you do with the money, Winston?"

"I converted it into diamonds before I left L.A."

"Smart. So where are they now?"

"In a safe-deposit box in Mexico City. I gave Ariel the key this afternoon when I tried to get her to make a run for it." Emory glared through the darkness at Matt. "The hut was burning down around us, but she wouldn't leave unless Chintalpa and I left. That's how decent and loyal she is. That's why I'd want to kill any son of a bitch that tried to hurt her.''

Matt took a deep breath. "I don't blame you. But we'll talk about Ariel later. Right now I want to know why you took the money."

Emory hesitated, then with a sigh he said, "I'd better start at the beginning."

"Take your time. We've got all night."

"It started when I tried to raise money to make *Winter Love*. I needed a lot more than the twenty-five million I got from Continental Trust. I was getting desperate, when a group of men from Chicago contacted me."

Emory told Matt what he'd told Ariel, about George Trevino and the Colombian drug cartel. "I tried to back out of the deal when I found out what they were up to," he said. "When I did, there was an accident on the set. One of the big lights fell. If it had hit one of the crew members, it would have been fatal. Trevino warned me there'd be more accidents. He said that maybe next time one of my principals would be hurt. He said maybe next time it would be Ariel."

"The bastard!"

"That's why I ran, McKay, and when I did I ran with *their* money, not Continental's. I figured they'd come after me and leave Ariel alone." Emory threw the half-smoked cigarette down and ground it under his heel. "What's left of Continental's money's in a numbered Swiss account along with a note that says if I don't show up in six months the money is to be transferred to the L.A. branch of Continental Trust."

"But you lost the Beverly Hills house," Matt said angrily. "You let it and everything else go." His hands curled into fists. "Do you have any idea what that did to Ariel? I was there, Winston. I know what she went through. She lost every damn thing she had in the world. All she kept was a music box that her mother had given her."

Emory ran a hand over his eyes. "But she's alive," he whispered. "I promised her mother I'd always take care of her and I always will. I'll do anything I have to to keep her safe. I'm sorry about the house, but better that than taking the chance of Trevino and his men getting their hands on her."

"They almost did today," Matt said. "Dammit, Winston, you should have gone to the FBI or to the police. They'd have given both of you round-the-clock protection. What kind of protection do you think you'll get here?" Matt looked around at the scattered huts. "There were only two men today, but you can bet that by tomorrow they'll have hired more men."

Matt began pacing up and down in the sand. "They'll find out your friend is a Chontal and track us down. It's only a matter of time. We've got to get out of here and back to L.A."

"You'll guarantee that Ariel will be protected if we go back?"

"You're damn right I will."

Emory nodded. "All right, McKay. You won't need your warrant." He glared at Matt. "Ariel told me about the warrants—one for me and one for her." He took a step closer to Matt. "Did you honestly believe that she was mixed up in this with me? How could you? How in the name of all that's holy could you?"

"I didn't. I mean after I knew what she was like, the kind of woman she is, I didn't." He looked at Emory through the darkness. "I'd never have used the warrant, Winston. You have to believe that."

"It doesn't matter what I believe," Emory said. "Ariel's the one you have to convince. And as for the warrant for my arrest, you won't need it. I'll go back with you, and I'll do what I should have done in the first place; I'll go to the authorities and I'll testify before a grand jury. There's nothing I want more than to see Trevino and the Colombians behind bars."

"Good." Some of Matt's anger dissipated. "But first I've got to get the two of you safely out of Mexico."

Emory nodded. "I have a feeling you know a lot more about these things than I do. Ariel and I will do whatever you say." Emory reached for another cigarette. "I gave these up two years ago when the doctor told me they weren't doing my heart any good. I started up again when the trouble with Trevino began. It's a rotten habit."

"I quit, too, but every time I get into a tight spot I automatically reach for one. That's why I don't carry them." Matt hesitated. "I suppose you want to talk about Ariel and me, about our relationship I mean."

"Yes, I do. And don't tell me to mind my own business. Ariel *is* my business. I love her."

"So do I." Matt took a deep breath and made himself go on. "At first I told myself it was just a job. She was the only lead we had; we figured she'd lead us to you."

Matt looked out toward the Gulf. By the light of the moon he could see the foam-covered whitecaps rolling in toward shore. He braced himself against the pain of going back to the beginning of his relationship with Ariel, but Winston had a right to know.

"At first I thought she was in on it with you. I was pretty convinced that she was when she asked me to come to Mexico with her." He leaned his back against one of the palms. "She asked me to come to Mexico because she thought I was a security agent. I suppose she figured I could take care of us if there was any trouble." He glanced at Emory. The other man's face was tense, waiting.

"We flew from L.A. to Acapulco," Matt went on. "There was a man at the airport there. He was watching Ariel. I hadn't spotted him before, but he must have been on the same flight we were on. He was one of the men shooting at you today."

"Did you tell Ariel about him?"

Matt shook his head.

"Why? Because you didn't trust her? Because you thought she already knew about him?"

"No. I didn't tell her because she was worn out, emotionally exhausted. She'd already been through too much. I didn't want to worry her."

"Did you see him again in Acapulco?"

"No, so I decided maybe I'd been imagining things, that he'd been staring at Ariel just because she's a beautiful woman."

"Yes, she is," Emory said. "And she's as good as she is beautiful."

Matt looked at Emory, then away. "We rented a car and drove from Acapulco to a place on the beach . . ."

The pain of remembrance made him stop. *And it was there we became lovers,* he thought. *It was there I first held Ariel in my arms, felt the whisper of her breath against my throat, felt her softness close in around me. . . .*

He forced himself to go on. "We took the road from Puerto Angel to Oaxaca," he said. "I noticed a car behind us. I slowed down, then speeded up. He stayed right on my tail. I lost him when he crashed against the side of the mountain. We made it into Oaxaca, and from there we started branching out, looking for you." He shoved himself away from the tree. "I didn't know that two of them had caught up with us until I found Ariel gone this morning. I checked downstairs at the hotel where we'd been staying. The—"

"Together?"

Matt's lips tightened. "Yes, together. The desk clerk told me that two men had checked in the night before. He said they'd asked what direction Ariel had taken. I ran back to the room and got my gun. I followed Ariel. I found her and your Indian friend, but before I could tell her about the two men the Indian slugged me."

"I'm glad he did." Emory reached for another cigarette, then with a shake of his head jammed the pack back into his pocket. "Let's walk," he said.

They went down to the beach and walked for a long time without speaking. Finally Emory said, "I'm trying not to like you, McKay. But you're a brave man, and I admire bravery. You saved our lives today." He stopped and looked at Matt. "But I'd like to beat the hell out of you for what you did to Ariel."

"Take your best shot if you think it'll make you feel any better."

"It won't." Emory looked out at the water. "Why didn't you tell her? When you knew what kind of a woman she was, how decent... Why didn't you tell her the truth?"

"I tried to." Matt's voice was strained with emotion. "But I was afraid to…afraid I'd lose her if I told her who I really was."

"You used her to get to me."

"In the beginning. That's not the way it became and that's not the way it is now. I'm in love with Ariel, and once we're safely out of here I'm going to do everything I can to make her trust me again. I want to marry her, Winston." Matt looked up at the slice of new moon overhead. "I can't imagine spending the rest of my life without her."

For a long time neither of them spoke. Finally Emory said, "If you mean that, McKay, then I hope that things'll work out. All I want in the world right now is Ariel's happiness." He took a deep breath. "And her safety." He held his hand out.

Together then, not quite friends but no longer enemies, the two of them walked back to the hut.

Ariel heard them come in together, but she didn't move.

Matt said, "Good night, Emory," and her stepfather whispered, "Sleep well."

She wondered what they had talked about. She'd told Emory earlier today that she and Matt had been lovers, and she'd seen his reaction. What had happened to make him change his mind about Matt?

Ariel stared up at the palm-frond roof, too tortured by her thoughts to sleep, too conscious of Matt lying only a few feet from her. If she had her way, she and Emory would leave here right now and make their own way back to California. But she knew they couldn't, not if the two men who'd tried to kill them today were still after them.

They would have to stay with Matt until they were safely out of Mexico. But once they were in California she'd never have to see him again.

Ariel turned her face to the bamboo wall and began to cry, silent tears for the love she had known, for the love she had lost.

When she awoke the next morning she was alone. A clean *huipil* lay folded next to the mat. Her body felt stiff from sleeping on the dirt floor, and when she sat up she groaned and rubbed one hip.

Sun slanted in through the beaded doorway, and the scent of wood smoke and coffee floated on the morning air.

She brushed her hair and fastened it with a clasp, then put the *huipil* on. Of a heavy white material, the dress was embroidered in brilliant colors of red, green and yellow around the square neck and the edge of the sleeves and skirt. She smoothed it down over her body, then hesitated, reluctant to go outside, where she knew she'd have to face Matt.

But when she stepped outside the hut she saw that Emory, bent over the brazier, was alone.

"Good morning, my dear," he said when he saw Ariel. "I like your dress." He indicated the loose dark shirt that he was wearing. "One of the villagers brought Matt and me the shirts and your dress this morning." He took a battered pot of coffee off the brazier, and when he poured some into a clay mug he handed it to her. "Tlalixa's wife sent over some cheese and tortillas. We'll eat just as soon as Matt returns."

He poured himself a cup of coffee, then said, "He went to take a look at Chintalpa. He'll change the bandage and make sure Chintalpa's all right." He looked at

Ariel, hesitated, then said, "We had a talk last night. I can't forgive or excuse what he did to you, Ariel, but I can understand that it was his job to find me."

"Any way he could," she said bitterly.

"I'm afraid so." Emory took a drink of his coffee. "He did a very brave thing yesterday, coming to our rescue the way he did. I think we must trust him to help us now."

"To take you back to stand trial?"

"I've agreed to go with him, Ariel. Matt'll see that the authorities prosecute the cartel, and I've agreed to testify before a grand jury."

Ariel's eyes went wide with shock. "But that's dangerous."

"Matt has assured me that both you and I will be protected. He—"

"*Matt* has assured you! My God, Emory, he's conning you the same way he conned me."

"I don't think so." Emory's expression grew more serious. "We're in grave danger, Ariel. The men who attacked the house yesterday won't give up. They know we escaped in the Jeep, and I'm sure they're out looking for us right now. Matt hid the Jeep early this morning. He thinks they'll probably hire more men to help them. He—" Emory stopped, smiling as Matt come toward them. "Good morning," he called out. "Ready for your breakfast?"

"More than ready. I could smell the coffee all the way from the *curandero*'s." He turned his gaze to Ariel. There were dark patches of fatigue under her eyes, and he knew that she hadn't slept any better than he had.

"How's Chintalpa this morning?" Emory asked.

"Better." Matt accepted the cup of coffee that Emory handed him. "His shoulder's stiff, but there isn't any infection. I'm pretty sure he's going to be all right." He put a piece of cheese into a tortilla and rolled it up. "I think we ought to get out of here as soon as we can, Emory. According to Tlalixa we're not too far from a place called Ixtaltepec. He says we can get a bus there that will take us in to Oaxaca."

"And from there?" Emory asked.

"We'll get a train or a plane to Mexico City." Matt looked at Ariel. "The painting you brought with you yesterday, is it of your mother?"

Ariel nodded. "Emory did it."

"It's very beautiful. She must have been a lovely woman. I know you'd like to take it with you, but I don't think we should."

"Why not?" Ariel bristled.

"We may run into trouble. It would be safer here. We can always come back for it."

"No," she said stubbornly. "I'm going to take it with me. I—" She stopped as a young man broke through the palms.

"Señores," he cried. "Tlalixa said you must go. A big car with six men approaches the village."

Emory shot a look at Matt. "They've come," he gasped.

Matt tensed. "Let's get the hell out of here. Get your bag, Ariel, but leave the painting."

She opened her mouth to argue, then turned and ran into the hut.

The young man looked anxious. "Hurry," he said. "I am to lead you out of here."

They heard the sound of an approaching car.

"Come!" He turned and ran toward the growth of jungle, the three of them only a few steps behind him.

Six men! Matt cursed under his breath and twisted an overhanging vine out of the way. Thank God he and Tlalixa had hidden the Jeep last night and that the villagers would make sure Chintalpa was safely hidden. They were good people. He prayed no harm would come to them.

Chapter 14

Instead of taking them into Salina Cruz, the young man led them to a strip of almost deserted beach. "Wait here until it is dark," he cautioned. "Do not try to go anywhere until then."

When he turned to leave, Matt grasped his arm. "Will you and your people be all right?" he asked.

"We are only poor Indians, some of us so dumb we can't even speak Spanish." The Chontal grinned. "Don't worry, *señor*," he said. "Our ancestors repulsed the Aztecs in the fifteenth century; surely today we can outsmart a few *gringos*."

Matt grinned back. "Tell your people how grateful we are for their help. And tell them we'll be back...." Matt looked at Emory. "That *Señor* Winston will be back when this is all over with. We left a painting in the hut where we stayed last night."

"I will take care of it."

"And the Jeep," Emory said. He handed the young man the key. "It shouldn't stand idle, *amigo*. I would consider it a favor if you used it as your own."

"All *right*!" The Indian's face lit up in a smile. Then the smile faded. "Be careful, my friends," he said. "I think these are very bad men who are after you."

The words echoed long after he had gone.

At the far end of the beach there was a stand that sold soft drinks and beer. Next to it some hammocks had been strung between a few palm trees. In the late afternoon a fisherman came down the beach with a fresh catch of fish. The woman who had the stand motioned Matt over and said that if he would buy the fish she would cook them.

After they had eaten and washed the fish down with lukewarm beer, Matt said, "It'll be dark soon. I'll go into town when it is and see about a bus."

"Do you still think we should go to Oaxaca?" Emory asked.

Matt shook his head. "Not now. Oaxaca would be the most logical place for us to get a direct flight or a train to Mexico City. It would be a better plan to head in the opposite direction, maybe go all the way up the Gulf of Mexico and head for Veracruz. It'll take us longer, but it's a safer bet."

Winston nodded. "Yes, I agree." He waited for Ariel to say something, but she only stared out at the water.

She lay in one of the hammocks, and when the two men began to talk she closed her eyes and pretended to sleep. She hated this sudden camaraderie between them. It was as though Emory had joined forces with Matt, as though he'd forgotten that Matt was his enemy, the man who had come to take him back to California.

She listened while they discussed the men in the Chicago-Colombian drug cartel. The name "Trevino" came up several times, and she remembered meeting a man by that name on the set of *Winter Love*. He'd been well groomed and ordinary-looking. He'd dressed conservatively, and his gray hair and mustache had been neatly trimmed. It was hard to believe he was the man who'd sent his goons after them.

"You and Ariel will be in protective custody until the trial is over," Matt said. "I've got a place in Santa Barbara. I'll arrange adequate protection, and you can stay there."

When hell freezes over, Ariel thought angrily. And finally, cooled by the breeze and lulled by their voices, she slept.

Matt was gone when she awoke. "He went in to Salina Cruz," Emory told her. "He's hoping there'll be a bus out of there tonight."

"Then I wish he'd take it."

"I know you're angry," Emory said. "I don't blame you, you have every right to feel the way you do. But we're in a precarious position, Ariel. McKay's smart. Did he tell you he was with Army Intelligence before he decided to become a banker? I have a feeling that if anybody can get us out of this alive, he can." He took her hand, and when he felt the tension there he said, "He's in love with you, Ariel. He wants to marry you."

She gave an unladylike snort.

"I can't forgive him for lying to you, but I can't help liking him, Ariel. He's a brave man, and we need him. It's important that we're a unit and that we follow Matt's orders. He got us away from Trevino's men the other day, but those same men are out looking for us now. God only knows what will happen if they find us. I made a terrible mistake by coming to Mexico. I should have . . .''

His voice rose as he talked, faster and faster. He became more agitated and began to rub his left arm.

"We have to be careful," he went on. "They're murderers, they're ruthless. Human life doesn't mean anything to them. They—"

Ariel rolled out of the hammock and went to him. "What's the matter with your arm?" she asked.

"Nothing." He shrugged as though whatever discomfort he'd been feeling wasn't important. But his face was pinched with pain. "You have to realize that we're in a serious situation, Ariel," he said urgently. "I have to know you'll follow Matt's orders."

Her lips tightened, but she saw the stress on her stepfather's face and said, "All right, Emory. The important thing is that we all get safely out of this. Matt and I are finished, but I promise you that I won't cause any problems."

"That's my girl." He smiled down at her, then said, just a bit too casually, "Think I'll take a little stroll."

He went down the beach to the shoreline. Ariel saw him rub his arm again, and a sudden feeling of fear shot through her. Two years ago Emory had been rushed to the hospital with what the doctor said was a mild heart attack. "You've had a warning," the cardiologist had told him. "You have to start taking it easy or one of these days you're going to have a real one."

Emory had been under a terrible strain for months. There'd been all of the production problems of *Winter Love*, then the knowledge of who the backers really were. For the past few weeks he'd lived with the knowledge that at any minute Trevino's hoods might catch up with him.

That alone was enough stress to last him a lifetime, but the attack on his place, the fire and the loss of his paintings, along with the flight through the jungle today, had taken their toll.

Ariel went to him. Linking her arm through his, she said, "Why don't you try to rest until Matt comes back?"

"Yes, perhaps I will." He sighed and turned away from the beach. "I love it here in Mexico," he said. "I hate the thought of going back to California."

"We'll come back, Emory. We'll find a house on the beach and you can paint." She hugged him. "I'm so sorry about your paintings."

"Yes, so am I. But I'm glad we saved the portrait of your mother, Ariel." He smiled down at her. "The older you get, the more you look like her. She was very beautiful, you know." He gazed out over the water. "The two of you changed my life. I didn't know how lonely I'd been until I met her. She was everything to me, Ariel, as you are now. I wanted to die when she died, but I had you. You were the reason I went on."

Ariel rubbed her cheek against his shoulder. "I don't know what I'd have done without you, Emory. I never thought of you as my stepfather. You were always my father. And I love you."

He kissed the top of her head. "And I love you, my dear."

When they went back to the hammocks, he lay down in one. "I was wrong to leave you, Ariel," he said. "Whatever my reasons, I was wrong to run away."

"It doesn't matter now. We're together and we're safe. We'll see this thing through until Trevino and his people are behind bars."

He sighed then and said, "I am rather tired. Perhaps I will rest for a while. Wake me when Matt returns."

"I will." Ariel kissed his forehead and sat beside him while he slept.

It was late when Matt returned. Ariel saw him coming down the beach and hurried to meet him.

"I'm worried about Emory," she said when she reached him. "I don't think he's feeling well."

"What's wrong?"

"He's been rubbing his left arm, and that scares me. He had a mild heart attack two years ago, and he was supposed to take it easy. But he was under so much stress with the film, and he started smoking again. He wasn't supposed to. He's not a young man. The last few days have been terrible for him. He's lost his house, his paintings." She shivered. "He almost lost his life, and now...now those men are after us."

Matt wanted to put his arms around her, but he knew that he couldn't. He wouldn't dare. He was grateful that she was even talking to him, and he hoped that meant she was willing to call a truce, if only until they were all safely out of Mexico.

"He's resting?" Matt asked.

Ariel nodded. "He's been sleeping for a couple of hours." She looked anxiously back at the hammock where Emory slept. "He should see a doctor," she said worriedly. "Maybe there's one in Salina Cruz."

"It's a small town, Ariel. There probably is a doctor, but I'm not sure how knowledgeable he'd be about a condition like Emory's." Matt hesitated. He didn't want to frighten her, but she had to be aware of the danger they were in.

"I honestly don't think we can risk staying in the area," he said. "The sooner we get out of here, the better. There's a bus leaving at midnight for a place called Matias Romero. From there, we change buses and head for the gulf coast." He looked at the luminous dial of his watch. "It's ten-thirty now. Emory can rest for a little while yet." He handed her a paper bag. "I bought some *tortas*, sandwiches and a few candy bars. Let's sit down."

Ariel looked at him, then quickly looked away. "I . . . I'd feel more comfortable near Emory."

"Then take a sandwich and a candy bar."

"No thanks."

"It's going to be a long night, Ariel. You'd better eat something."

"All right." She looked at him again. "Thank you," she said before she turned away.

Matt watched her. He knew she was scared, not so much of the men who were looking for them as she was about Emory. His brows came together in a worried frown. He hoped Ariel was mistaken in her concern for her stepfather. There were dangerous men after them; this would be a hell of a time for Emory to get sick.

He refused to think the words "heart attack."

He could see the outline of her figure sitting on the sand next to Winston. He knew how frightened she was and how alone she felt at this moment. He wanted to go to her, to take her in his arms and comfort her. He wished he'd never lied to her. He wished he could take her away from here, somewhere where she'd always be safe.

At eleven-fifteen he woke Winston. The older man seemed tired, but he insisted he felt perfectly all right. They took their time walking to Salina Cruz and arrived at the bus station a few minutes before the third-class bus for Matias Romero left.

Because of the hour, there were not many people leaving Salina Cruz, only a few ranchers who'd come in for a night on the town, several families and one or two businessmen. For the first half hour the ranchers sang along with the driver's radio and passed a bottle of tequila among themselves. But in a little while they quieted down and went to sleep.

Heat and dust blew in from the open window. The bus driver's radio blared, and somewhere in the back of the bus a child began to cry.

But Emory managed to sleep. Ariel had insisted he take the seat next to the window so that he'd be away from the up and down commotion of the ranchers and of the few passengers who flagged the bus down from the highway from time to time.

She didn't even try to sleep, and neither did Matt, who'd taken the seat across the aisle from them. He was worried. If the two men who'd set fire to Emory's place had recruited four others so quickly, chances were they could recruit more men just as fast. They might even have the bus stations watched. Two *gringos* and a young blond woman would be easy to spot. He and Winston were wearing Indian shirts, but they were obviously North Americans. Ariel too was wearing an Indian dress, but with her hair they'd spot her three blocks away.

Matt swung around. A family, mother and father, three younger children and a teenage boy, were sitting in the long seat in the back of the bus. Both the father and the older son were wearing broad-brimmed straw hats.

Matt thought for a moment, then he got up and went back to speak to them.

"*Buenas noches,*" he said softly, so that he wouldn't awaken the children. "*Perdón la molestia*, but would it be possible to buy your straw hats, *señor*?"

"*Los sombreros?*" The man looked startled. "But, *señor*, why would you want the *sombreros*? They are old. You can buy much better ones in any market."

"I can't explain, but I have need of them now." Matt took two twenty-dollar bills out of his back pocket. "I would like to buy your wife's *rebozo* also."

The man looked at the money, then at his wife. "Give me your *rebozo, vieja*, old woman," he said.

His wife, who had been half asleep, looked at her husband. She pulled the baby she was holding closer. "You want my *rebozo*?" she asked sleepily.

"The *señor* wants to buy it. I will buy you another one tomorrow." He pulled it off her shoulders and handed it to Matt. And without waking his son he took the boy's straw hat and gave it to Matt, then his own. With a laugh he said, "Is there anything else, *señor*? One of my children, perhaps?"

Matt laughed with him, then tousled one of the sleeping children's hair. "No, *amigo*, though I'm sure they're very fine children." He offered his hand. "*Gracias, señor, muchas gracias.*"

Back in his seat, Matt gave the dark shawl to Ariel. "I want you to put this on before we leave the bus," he told her. "Make sure when you do that your hair is covered."

"But you said that if we came this way we'd be safe."

"No, I said the men would be less likely to look for us in this direction. But I can't be sure, Ariel. They might have men covering the bus stations. When we get to where we change buses I'll get off with the ranchers. You and Emory hang back with one of the families. I'll find out when the bus for the coast leaves, and when it does the two of you follow me on."

She looked scared again, and because he knew he could not touch her, he said, "You'd better try to get some sleep."

"That's not easy to do with the driver's radio blaring."

"Maybe it helps keep him awake. It—"

The blare of music stopped, and a voice came on to advertise Colgate, pronounced Col-ga-tay, toothpaste. That was followed by a commercial for laundry soap and a weather announcement.

Matt leaned forward, listening. "Damn," he muttered when the music started up again, "that's just what we needed."

"What is it?"

"A hurricane's building up just east of Cuba."

"A hurricane?"

"Headed for the same coast we're heading for." And it was a vulnerable coast. A couple of years ago a hurricane had hit the Yucatán with winds over a hundred-and-twenty-five miles an hour. It had marooned tourists in Cozumel and Cancun and destroyed homes in half of the coastal towns. Another storm, ten or twelve years ago, almost wiped out Ciudad del Carmen. The whole gulf coast, from the Yucatán to Tampico, was wide open to every vicious storm that came blowing in off the Caribbean.

Matt tried not to let his apprehension show. Ariel had enough to worry about. "There's a lot of water out there," he said with a forced smile. "Most of the hurricanes that originate near Cuba hit the Florida coast.

Anyway, it's a couple of days away. Once we get to Veracruz it's less than a day's trip to Mexico City. If the hurricane does veer toward Mexico, we'll be out of the region before it hits.'' He pretended to yawn and said, ''We'd better get some sleep.''

But Matt didn't sleep. He worried about the storm, about the men who were out there somewhere looking for them, and about Emory. If Winston had a heart attack and they weren't able to go on, they'd be sitting ducks.

He looked over at Ariel, and though she pretended to sleep he knew she was as awake, as tense, as he was. He wanted to reach out and take her hand, to tell her how much he loved her. But all he could do was breathe a silent prayer for her safety.

They reached Matias Romero a little after three in the morning. Ariel awakened Emory. He put the straw hat on, and she put the *rebozo* over her head and around her shoulders. When the bus stopped, Matt jostled his way in among the sleepy ranchers. He threw his arm around one man's shoulders and the man handed him a half-empty bottle of tequila. Matt drank, and in a drunken voice said, ''*Gracias, mi hermano,* my brother.''

Ariel and Emory waited until the family Matt had bought the straw hats and the shawl from passed, then fell in behind them. One of the little boys turned around to stare at Ariel. The rest of his family got off first, and when his father turned back to lift the little boy, Ariel said, ''I'll get him,'' and picking the child up in her arms, she got off the bus.

Still holding the child, she darted a quick glance around the small station. She didn't see Matt, and for an instant fear closed in around her. What if he'd left them? What if ... No, there he was, slouched against one wall, a bottle of tequila in his hand, the straw hat pulled low over his face.

The family with the little boy said something to her in Spanish. She didn't understand, and Emory, with a smile to the family, translated, ''They're going toward the coast, too, so we'll probably be taking the same bus.''

''How long do we have to wait for it?'' she whispered.

Emory asked the man, then to Ariel said, ''About an hour and a half.''

The little boy shifted in her arms. His mother said something to him, and he shook his head.

''She's afraid he's bothering you,'' Emory said. ''I assured her that you loved children and that he wasn't bothering you at all.''

''Of course he isn't.''

It occurred to Ariel then that with the *rebozo* covering her hair and the child on her lap she could pass for an Indian woman, which was exactly what she wanted to do. She lowered her head against the child's and darted a glance around the room to see if anyone was watching her. When she was sure no one was she closed her eyes and pretended to sleep.

But someone was watching. Matt had spotted the man as soon as he'd stepped off the bus. A dark fellow of medium height, dressed in cheap modern clothes, he'd been pretending to read a newspaper, but he'd checked each person out as they got off the bus.

He was sitting in one of the cramped seats, still pretending to read a newspaper, but his eyes kept scanning the room. He looked toward Ariel. She bent toward the child, and Matt heaved a sigh of relief when the man's gaze moved on. Then the little boy shifted in Ariel's lap.

He reached up, and before Ariel could stop him he tugged on the *rebozo*. One side of it fell back.

"*Rubia*, blond," the boy said, and curled a strand of her hair around his finger.

The man swung around. He stared at Ariel, then turned and headed for the phone just inside the ticket booth.

Matt shoved away from the wall. He lurched against the man, intercepting him, and mumbled, "*Perdóname.*" He draped an arm across the stranger's shoulder and, singing loudly, propelled him away from the ticket booth, toward the door.

The man protested and tried to pull away. Matt jammed an elbow into his ribs, then found a vulnerable nerve in the shoulder cord and squeezed hard. The man cried out, but Matt covered the cry with his singing.

Once outside Matt yanked the man around the side of the building, away from the station lights. The streets were deserted. The man tried to pull away. He kicked, aiming for Matt's groin, and at almost the same time reached down and pulled a knife out of his boot. Matt dodged the kick and brought the flat of his hand down hard against the back of his opponent's neck. When he sagged, Matt grabbed him and pulled him into the alleyway behind the bus station. He took the flowered tie from around the man's neck, bound his hands with it, then shoved the crumpled pocket handkerchief into his mouth and dragged the limp form behind a pile of trash.

When Matt stepped out of the alleyway he checked his watch. They still had over an hour before the bus they wanted came in. He didn't want to wait around that long.

He went back into the bus station. The bus they'd just gotten off of had started up. He ran up to it just as the door closed.

"A dónde va?" he called out.

The bus driver opened the door. "To San Lorenzo, *señor*. The bus you want will be here in an hour or so."

"Wait! We will go with you." Matt ran back into the station. "Hurry!" he called to Emory.

Emory looked up, startled. Then he took Ariel's arm. "Come," he said urgently.

She hesitated only a moment, then handed the little boy she'd been holding to his father. *"Adiós,"* she said and hurried out of the station with Emory.

The bus driver gunned his motor. "Come on if you're coming," he growled.

Matt helped Emory and Ariel to board. The long back seat was empty, and they headed for it, holding onto the backs of seats when the bus lurched out of the driveway.

"What happened?" Emory asked when they sat down. His face, in the light of the passing streetlights, looked ghastly pale.

"I think he was one of their men, somebody they hired to watch the bus station."

"They'll be watching the other stations, too, then." Ariel looked frightened. "What are we going to do?"

"Try to hit the smaller towns. Stick to second or third-class buses. As far as I can tell by the map it looks like San Lorenzo is a small place. We'll find a hotel and stay there during the day. Tonight we'll go on to the coast." He studied Emory's face. "We all need a decent meal and a good rest," he said.

And tried not to think about the approaching hurricane.

* * *

There was one hotel in San Lorenzo. Because he wanted to keep his eye on Emory, Matt suggested that he and the older man share a room. "It's better not to spread out too much," he said. "And Ariel will be right next door."

They ate scrambled eggs laced with chili, boiled beans and tortillas for breakfast. Emory barely touched his food.

Matt's eyes met Ariel's across the table. Because he knew how worried she was, he said, "I'm about done in. What do you say we go to bed as soon as we finish breakfast?"

"Yes," she said quickly. "I'm awfully tired. What about you, Emory?"

He rubbed a weary hand across his face. "I could do with some sleep," he said. He covered her hand with his. "This trouble we're in, it's all my fault, Ariel. I should never have left California. I should have sent you away and gone to the FBI. I thought I was protecting you, but all I've done is put you in danger, you and Matt."

"But we're going to be all right." Ariel looked at Matt. "Where do we go from here?" she asked.

"I've been checking the map. If we can get a bus to San Andrés Tuxtla, we'll go there, then on to Veracruz. And once in Veracruz, we're home free." He smiled reassuringly. "We take a plane to Mexico City, pick up the diamonds and grab the first flight out to L.A."

For Emory's sake, and to prove to herself that she wasn't really frightened, Ariel said, "And a big plate of pasta at the Scandia."

"Or margaritas at Rick's Cafe Américain." Matt looked across the table at her.

"Rick's?" Emory raised a questioning eyebrow. "Don't think I know the place."

"It's new," Matt said, still looking at Ariel. "Done in a Casablanca-type setting. They even have a piano player by the name of Sam."

"And of course he plays 'As Time Goes By'." Emory smiled at Ariel. "That's the tune of your music box, isn't it, dear?"

"Yes." Ariel tried to keep her voice steady. She remembered then that she'd left the music box back in the room the morning she'd run away from Matt. But it didn't matter because she knew she'd never want to hear its tinny melody again.

"Your mother loved that song. And Bogart. He was the only man I was ever jealous of, even though I used to try to imitate him."

"Yes, so did I." Matt caught Ariel's gaze again. "Do you remember, Ariel?"

"I remember." Her eyes shone with unshed tears. She tried to tear her gaze from his, and couldn't. The fragments of the melody, the words of the song, ran round and round in her head . . . a kiss is still a kiss . . .

She pushed her chair back from the table. "I'm awfully tired," she said. "I've got to . . . to rest."

Then she turned and ran from the room.

Neither man spoke. Finally Emory said, "She's still in love with you."

Matt swallowed hard. "But will she ever forgive me?"

Emory shook his head. "I don't know, Matt," he said softly. "But for both your sakes I hope that someday she will."

Matt paid the check then, and they went down the hall to their room. Emory lay down on one of the twin beds and fell asleep almost immediately.

But it was a long time before Matt went to sleep. And when he did it was to dream of Ariel, and how it had been between them in the beginning.

"You must remember this," she said in his dream. "A kiss is still a kiss...."

He reached for her, but when he awoke she wasn't there.

He slept again, and the next time he awoke he could hear the rain beating against the windows.

The storm had started kicking up its heels.

Chapter 15

It was raining hard by the time they left San Lorenzo that night. Thunder rumbled down off the mountains, and lightning split a jagged pathway through the sky. The road, already rutted and filled with potholes, became a jarring, dangerous nightmare.

Most of the passengers got off at stops along the way. Only a few got on. They all looked worried.

Clinging to the backs of the seats, Matt made his way to the front of the bus. "What's the latest weather report?" he asked the driver, raising his voice to be heard over the crackling static of the radio.

"It's one lousy *cabrón* of a storm," the driver said. "It knocked the hell out of Cuba, now it's coming across the Gulf straight toward Mexico."

"What are the winds like?"

"More than one hundred and thirty miles an hour, *señor*. With gusts up to one-fifty."

"Has the weather bureau pinpointed where it'll hit?"

"Somewhere between Campeche and Tampico." The driver took his eyes off the road for a moment and looked at Matt. "We're going to get the hell knocked out of us," he said.

"Wouldn't it be better to stop? Before we get to the coast, I mean?"

"There's nothing much between here and there, only a few villages. I've got a wife and seven kids in San Renaldo. That's on the coast, and that's where we're heading. It's a small town, but there's a decent hotel there. Unless the storm gets too bad, it's safe enough." The radio crackled again. He played with the dial, got only scrambled static, and cursed.

"You and your family and the rest of the passengers can check into the hotel or maybe take refuge in one of the churches," he said.

A gust of wind hit the bus, and the driver tightened his hands on the wheel. Suddenly the static cleared, and a voice said, "The latest advisory..." The voice faded out, then in. "The storm is traveling at a rate of ten kilometers an hour. At its present rate of speed it will hit the coast, somewhere between Campeche and Veracruz, by..."

The voice faded. The driver smacked the side of the radio. "...a dangerous storm. All precautions must be taken. Those in the coastal area are urged to find higher ground by..."

The radio crackled and the voice faded.

"How long before we get there?" Matt asked.

"In this weather? *Quién sabe?*"

Matt made his way back up the aisle. Because the bus wasn't crowded, Ariel and Emory had moved to seats midway on the bus and were clinging to the seat in front of them to keep from being jarred into the aisle.

"What's happening with the storm?" Emory asked. "The radio sounded garbled from back here."

"Most of it was." For a moment Matt hesitated, wondering how much he should tell them and whether or not he should soften the news. But he decided to give it to them straight.

"The storm is bad," he said. "It's hurricane force, with winds up to one-thirty, and it's headed just about where we're going."

"When will it hit?" Emory asked.

"I'm not sure. We couldn't make it out." Matt took the empty seat across the aisle. "The driver isn't going to attempt to make it all the way to Veracruz. We're going to a place called San Renaldo. He said there was a hotel there." He looked at Ariel, trying to reassure her. "We're going to be all right," he said.

"That depends on how sturdy the hotel is, doesn't it?" Emory forced a laugh. "I was in a hurricane in Miami once. Sat it out in a frat house at the university there when I was a junior. We had a couple of bottles of rum, a transistor radio and some of the girls from one of the sororities. Had ourselves a hell of a time."

"I don't know about the girls," Matt said. "But maybe we can find a bottle of rum if—"

The bus hit a rut, skidded, then lurched forward. Rain slashed hard against the windows.

"How long . . ." Ariel wet her lips. "How long before we get to where we're going?"

"I'm not sure. Why don't you try to get some rest?"

"Rest?" She pulled the *rebozo* closer around her shoulders. "You've got to be kidding." She closed her hand over Emory's and asked, "How are you feeling?"

"Fine," he said quickly. "But I'll be glad to get somewhere safe."

Ariel looked at Matt, and he could see the concern in her face. "Yes, so will I," he said.

But it was almost morning before the bus pulled into the little town of San Renaldo. The wind had grown stronger, and the rain beat with punishing force as the passengers scrambled out of the bus and into the one-room station.

"The hotel is just down the street," the bus driver told everybody when they got inside. "And there's a church right next door. Either place'll be better than sitting here once the hurricane hits."

The passengers looked at one another. Some of them said, "Let's go to the church," and two or three said they would try the hotel.

"We'd better go to the hotel, too," Matt said.

Ariel linked her arm through Emory's. "Yes, I agree. We might as well be comfortable."

Matt went to the door and tried to see through the blinding rain.

"The hotel is at the end of the street, *señor*," the man who was closing the ticket office said. "On your right, down near the water."

"Down near the...!" Matt swore under his breath. "I'm afraid we've got to make a run for it," he told Ariel. He took the straw hat off and reached for Emory's. "We won't need these, and they won't stay on in this wind, anyway." He tossed them onto one of the seats. "Okay," he said. "Let's go."

They were soaked to the skin as soon as they stepped out of the doorway. The driving rain slashed at their bodies as, arms linked, heads bent hard into the wind, they struggled to the hotel.

The front windows of the two-story hotel had been boarded up. The lobby, lighted by candles, was small and crowded with people.

"We lost our lights a little while ago," the man behind the desk told them. "But there are candles in all of the rooms." He looked at the three of them. "I presume the three of you want a room?"

"Rooms," Matt said. "Three, if you have them."

"I'm afraid I don't have three, but I do have one room. It has two beds. Will that do?"

"It'll have to." Matt wiped the rain off his face. "We're soaked through," he said. "When do the stores open?"

"I doubt they will, *señor*. But very likely the market will open for a few hours. You'll be able to buy something there."

Matt signed the register, and the man handed him a key. "Your room is upstairs, *señor*. In the back. It's really a lovely view of the Gulf...." He stopped, then chuckled and said, "Well, not today, of course. But I'm sure you'll find it quite satisfactory." He handed Matt a package of matches. "For the candles," he said.

They started up the stairway.

Halfway up Emory stopped. "Wait," he gasped, "I can't..."

"What is it?" Ariel put an arm around him.

"I don't know. I..." He slumped against her and would have fallen if Matt hadn't grabbed him and eased him down to a step.

"What's the matter, Winston?"

"Chest. Seem to be having...difficulty breathing. Pain." He clutched his chest. "Hell of a pain."

"Tell the man at the desk," Matt said to Ariel.

"But—"

"Do it now! Ask if there's a doctor. Find out where the hospital is."

She ran down the steps. In less than a minute she was back with the man from the front desk.

"There is a Social Security Hospital, *señor*," he told Matt. "I have a car. We will take the gentleman."

"Thank you." Matt helped Emory to rise. "Can you make it or do you want me to try to get an ambulance?"

"I can make it." Emory leaned on Matt. His face was the color of paste. "Hell of a nuisance. Sorry."

"Don't be silly."

With Ariel's help, Matt eased Emory down the steps and out of the hotel into the car. Her face had gone as pale as Emory's. "How far is the hospital?" she asked.

"Just outside of town, *señorita*. We will be there in a few minutes. If it were not for this terrible weather..." He shook his head and tightened his hands on the steering wheel.

The hospital stood at the rise of a small hill. When the hotel man, who told them his name was *Señor* Lopez, stopped, Matt ran in. "We have an emergency," he said in Spanish to the nurse behind the desk. "We need a stretcher."

She looked at him, didn't ask questions, then barked something into the phone. A couple of minutes later two orderlies appeared with a litter.

Things happened quickly then, for although the hospital was small it seemed to be efficiently run.

Matt and Ariel were told to wait while Emory was wheeled into an emergency room.

Ariel, tense and frightened, paced the narrow waiting room. "This has been too much for him," she said. "He's been through so much. His heart isn't strong." She stopped pacing. "It's a heart attack, isn't it?" she asked Matt. "The hospital's so small. I bet there isn't even a cardiologist in town. If we'd only been in a bigger city. If—"

"Take it easy," Matt said. Her body was taut with tension, her face strained and pale. Like him, her clothes were soaked through, and her wet hair hung in tangled strands down her back. He wanted to go to her, to hold and comfort her. But he knew he couldn't, that even now she wouldn't accept any comfort he had to offer.

Finally an intern, who looked much too young to be a doctor, came out to speak to Matt and Ariel.

"Because of the storm many of our staff have been alerted to be on duty today," he told them. "But we don't have a cardiologist. We are close enough to Veracruz, and when we have a heart case we send the patient there by ambulance. But that is out of the question because of the storm."

"But why?" Ariel asked frantically. "The roads are still open, aren't they? We could—"

"The highway to Veracruz is closed, *señorita*. But please, do not worry. I have ordered a blood test and a cardiogram for *Señor* Winston. It will be a little while before I have the results, but meantime our resident physician is with him. I assure you he will have the best of care."

Ariel's face showed her fear. "Is it a heart attack?"

"We cannot say until after the cardiogram." A nurse signaled the young man, and he said, "I am sorry, but you must excuse me now. We are making preparations for the hurricane. People will be hurt, we must have everything ready."

Thirty minutes went by before an older doctor came out to speak to them. "*Señor* Winston is resting now," he said.

"It's his heart, isn't it?" Ariel asked anxiously. "He's had a heart attack, hasn't he?"

"Certainly his heart is affected. He seems to be under a great deal of stress. He needs rest, and I have given him a sedative. But it is not a heart attack."

Relief washed over Ariel, and she said, "Can I see him?"

"He is resting now. It would be best not to disturb him." A gust of wind hit the building, and he said, "Perhaps he will sleep through the storm."

"I'd like to stay here with him."

The doctor shook his head. "I am sorry, but that won't be possible. This is a small hospital, and I am afraid that soon we will be flooded with injured. It would be better if you went to the hotel or to the church." He looked at his watch. "And very soon. The hurricane is due to arrive within the next hour or two."

"But I don't want to leave!"

When she looked up at Matt for support he took her arm and said, "The doctor's right, Ariel. We'd only be in the way here." And to the doctor he added, "We have a room at the hotel. We'll check back as soon as the storm passes."

"Very good, *señor*. You and the *señorita* must change into dry clothes as soon as you can. And have her try to get some rest. The storm will last for many hours."

"And I must get back to the hotel," *Señor* Lopez said. "I left my wife in charge, but she is a very nervous woman. She doesn't like to be left alone, especially when a storm like this is on the way."

Matt thanked the doctor, then he gently, but firmly, led Ariel out of the hospital.

The wind had picked up while they'd been inside, and the hotel owner's car swayed dangerously as he slowly drove back to the hotel through the pounding rain.

Matt asked to be let off at the town market. "You go on up to the room," he told Ariel. "I'll be there just as soon as I can get us some dry clothes." And to *Señor* Lopez he said, "You've been very kind, *señor*. If you need help during the storm, please don't hesitate to tell me. I'll be glad to help in any way I can."

Ariel watched him run through the rain into the covered market. Chilled through, she shivered, and knew how cold and damp Matt must feel.

She too thanked *Señor* Lopez, then hurried to the room on the second floor. Two boards had been criss-crossed over the window, and she went to stand there and look out at the Gulf of Mexico.

Palm trees bent double. Palm fronds and pieces of de-bris blew wildly about. Twelve-foot waves pounded the shore. Each time one of them hit, it was as though a giant fist shook the hotel. What would happen when the full force of the storm was upon them? Ariel wondered. Could the hotel withstand the hurricane winds? Could the hospital? She thought of Emory and prayed that he would be safe and that the doctor had been right in his diagnosis.

At last she went into the bathroom. She took off her wet clothes and hung them on the shower curtain, and when she got into the old-fashioned tub she turned on the shower and quickly bathed and washed her hair, wishing the water was hot. When she got out, she wrapped herself in one of the towels.

It seemed to her that the wind was stronger when she came back into the room, and she went to stand by the window, drawn by the power of the approaching storm.

She was still standing there when Matt returned. He came in, dripping water on the tiled floor, and handed Ariel a plastic-wrapped package.

"I'll go take a shower," he said, wiping his rain-wet hair back from his face. He looked at her, clad only in the towel that barely covered her from the rise of her breasts to the apex of her legs. Her fair hair hung in damp, wispy curls around her shoulders, and he felt an overwhelming need to pull her into his arms.

He turned away before he did. "I hope you'll find something that'll fit you," he said, indicating the package. "I bought some fruit, too. The hotel dining room won't open during the storm."

Inside the plastic bag there was another bag filled with fruit: apples, bananas and a papaya. In another bag there were two pairs of *guaraches* and two sweatshirts, one with "Cancun" printed on the front, the other with Mickey Mouse.

Ariel opted for the mouse.

There were also two pairs of blue jeans. The smaller, boys' size, fit. She put the clothes on, then knocked on the bathroom door and said, "I'm putting your clothes on the doorknob."

"Okay," Matt called out. "Thanks."

She closed the door, then looked around the room that they were sharing. It was a small room with a double bed, a single bed and an old-fashioned dresser. She took one of the apples, sat down on the double bed and looked out at the storm.

She was still sitting there when Matt came out of the bathroom. "Our clothes should be dry by a week from Saturday," he said. He handed her a bright yellow transistor radio that he'd had in his pants' pocket. "I picked this up, too. And a flashlight. I thought they might come in handy."

"What time is it?" Ariel asked.

"Almost two. *Señor* Lopez said the dining room would be closing soon. We'd better have something to eat while we still have a chance."

They ate ham and eggs, the only food that was left in the hotel kitchen, and tried not to look at each other across the candlelit table. Matt knew how worried she was about Winston, and about the storm. He knew she didn't like the idea of being alone with him, and he understood when she lingered over her coffee, reluctant to leave the small dining room.

When they went through the lobby they saw that it was filled with even more people who, like themselves, were refugees from the storm. The front door, as well as the windows, were boarded up now.

"The storm is almost here," *Señor* Lopez said. "The hotel has withstood other hurricanes, it will withstand this one." A gust of wind hit. He glanced at the boarded-up windows nervously. "I am sure it will. It's a strong building. It..." He wet his lips and tried to force a smile. "I will see you tomorrow when it is over, yes?"

"Yes, of course," Matt said. He took hold of Ariel's arm and felt her trembling.

They went up the stairs together, and when they were in the room, Matt said, "It might be a good idea to try to get some sleep before the storm really hits." He indicated the double bed that was farthest from the window. "Why don't you take that? I'll stretch out on the other one."

"Yes, all right."

"Would you like me to light one of the candles?"

"No. We...we might need it later." She took the *guaraches* off and lay down. "Do you think Emory will be all right?" she asked.

"Yes, I'm sure the doctor knew what he was talking about. Emory's been under a lot of stress, he needs a good rest, and he'll get it in the hospital. We won't leave until the doctor is sure that it's safe for him to travel."

"And what about the stress when we go back?" She faced him. "When you take us back?"

"It won't be all that bad. I told you, you and Emory will stay at my place in Santa Barbara. He'll only have to come in to L.A. to testify." Matt sat down on the other bed, facing her. "Can we have a talk, Ariel? About us, I mean."

"Not now."

"But I..."

She rolled onto her side away from him.

"All right." Matt sighed. "But we will talk about this, Ariel, because no matter what you think of me, I *do* love you." He waited, and when she didn't answer, he said, "And I think you love me."

She put her fist against her mouth to keep from crying out. All she wanted in the world right now was to lift her arms to him, to have him come down beside her, to hold her and love her and make the storm go away.

But Ariel didn't move, or speak. And finally, tears staining her cheeks, she fell into a troubled sleep.

The window shattered with a crash.

Ariel came awake, a scream on her lips. "What . . . ? What is it?" she cried.

Matt was on his feet, the flashlight in his hand. "Stay where you are," he ordered. "There's broken glass everywhere."

And rain, blowing through the broken window with a terrible force.

He came to her. "Hold the flashlight," he said over the roar of the wind. "Point it over here." He pushed the old-fashioned dresser toward the window, shoved it over on its side, then in front of the window. The wind still whistled in, but it blocked most of the rain.

"Are you all right?" Matt crossed the room to her.

"Yes. I . . . This is it, isn't it? The storm?"

"I'm afraid so. We'd better put the bed as far from the window as it'll go."

Ariel started to get up, but he said, "No, stay where you are," and pushed the bed against the far wall. He stood for a moment then, uncertain about what to do next, wondering how he could allay her fear. "I hope you don't mind the darkness," he said. "We can't risk lighting the candles because of the wind."

He sat down on the bed next to her and took the radio out of his pants' pocket. "Maybe we can get some news."

He fiddled with it, found static, then finally picked up a voice speaking in rapid Spanish.

"What is it?" Ariel asked. "What is he saying?"

"Wait a minute." Matt listened, and when the weather report finished, he switched the radio off. "We're getting the direct force of the storm now," he told Ariel. "Estimated winds are over one hundred and thirty miles an hour, gusts up to one-sixty. The waves are high, cresting at—"

Something smashed against the side of the building. Ariel cried out, and without thinking she grabbed at Matt.

"It's okay." He put his arms around her, holding his breath, half expecting her to push him away. But she didn't, she clung to him, her face burrowed against his shoulder, clutching him when a blast of wind shook the building.

"Do you think the hotel is sturdy enough? Do you think it can stand up under the wind?"

"*Señor* Lopez said it's been through other hurricanes. It'll be all right, Ariel."

"What about the water? What if the water rises? What if..." She shook her head. "I'm sorry. I'm acting like a baby. Forgive me."

She tried to pull away from him, but Matt held her. "A hurricane can be a pretty scary thing," he said. "Especially when you're right on the beach in a hotel like this one. But we're going to be all right, honey. Take it easy."

Ariel felt his lips brush the top of her head. She told herself to move away, but his arms felt so good, so strong. They were a shelter from the storm... A gust hit with terrible force. She smothered a scream against Matt's shoulder. "Hold me," she cried. "Hold me."

His arms closed tightly around her. "It's all right," he soothed. "Don't be afraid, Ariel. Don't be afraid, love."

She raised her face to his, trying to see him in the darkness of the room. "Matt," she whispered, "Oh, Matt, I—"

He stopped her words with a kiss that shook him like the wind that roared in through the broken window. Everything that he'd been feeling since that morning she had run away from him, all of the fear and the anger, the hunger, and the hopelessness that she would never love him again, surged to the surface. He crushed her to him, his mouth hard and urgent against hers.

She broke away. She said, "No, don't—" But when his mouth found hers again her lips softened and parted, and her arms crept around him, then tightened to hold him as he was holding her.

And suddenly it didn't matter that the storm raged all around them or that rain slashed in through the broken window. She was here with Matt, being held by him, kissed by him. And when he laid her back against the pillow, she pulled him down beside her, as hungry as he was now, wanting to be possessed by him, covered and filled by him.

She felt his hands slip up under the sweatshirt, and when he cupped her breasts she cried out in her pleasure and said, "Yes, oh yes, Matt."

He helped her to sit up so that he could pull the shirt over her head, then quickly struggled out of his.

When they were together again, he cupped one of her breasts in his hand and began to lap it with his tongue, and when she quivered at his touch and threaded her fingers through the darkness of his hair, holding him there, offering herself, he thought his body would burst with pleasure.

He stopped to take her jeans off, but when he began to unfasten his she said, "No, let me."

She eased him back on the bed while she unzipped them and began to tug them down over his hips. For a moment she rested the palm of her hand against his stomach, then lower. And when she felt his arousal, the breath caught in her throat and she whispered, "Hurry. Oh, hurry, Matt."

He threw the jeans aside and came up over her. For a moment he rested his body against hers, then with a low cry he raised himself up and joined his body to hers.

They moved together, straining and close, as wild as the storm that raged all about them. Her warmth and her softness shielded him; his strength and his body protected her.

They clung together, whispering each other's names. He sought her mouth, and they kissed. She lifted her body to his, and he murmured, "Yes, love. Like that, love."

The storm and the wind that rocked the frail building didn't matter now, nor did the waves that licked at the foundation. They were one for this brief period of time. They had found their shelter in each other's arms.

Chapter 16

When Ariel awoke the next morning she listened for the wind. But the wind had died, and the only sound was the slow, steady roll of the waves against the shore. She opened her eyes and saw the sun streaming through the broken window where only shattered pieces of glass remained. Even the boards had been blown away by the storm. The curtains were torn and wet, debris littered the floor.

Matt lay with his body pressed close to hers, his arm across her waist, one leg between hers. They had made love last night while the storm raged all around them. Clinging and close, they'd shut out the sound of the rain and of the wind that had threatened to topple the hotel and hurl them into the sea. Time after time Matt had carried her on a high crest of passion unlike anything she had ever known. They slept, and then woke to love again. Her body was sore, her muscles ached from the loving.

No, not loving, she told herself as she moved out of his embrace, from *making* love. There was a difference.

Matt reached for her. "Where ya goin'?" he murmured.

"I'm getting up."

"Not yet." He stretched and groaned. "Call the paramedics," he said. "I'm ruined. I may never be able to walk again." He opened his eyes and grinned. "What did you do to me last night, woman?"

"The storm has passed," she said. "It's morning."

"That it is. And I'm in need of sustenance. C'm'ere and give me a kiss."

"Matt, please..." She took a steadying breath. "What happened last night—"

"Many, many times last night."

"Shouldn't have happened."

He raised one dark eyebrow.

"It doesn't change anything." She pulled part of the sheet up to cover her nakedness. "Whatever it was we thought we had—"

"*Thought* we had?"

Ariel nodded. "Thought we had. It's over. It ended when I knew why you'd really come to Mexico with me, when I found the warrants and knew you'd only used me to get to Emory."

"But last night..." Matt braced himself against the pain her words were causing. "We made love last night, Ariel," he said at last. "We were one person. You can't deny what we felt, the passion that we shared."

"I don't deny it, Matt," she said carefully. "The passion is there, I know that. But that's all it is now."

"You're wrong." He felt as though he were drowning, as though he would drown if he couldn't find the right words. "I love you," he said.

"And I loved you. Maybe I still do." She turned away from him. "But even that isn't enough to build a relationship on, Matt. There has to be trust, and we . . . you didn't have that. From the very beginning you didn't trust me. Even afterward, when we . . . when we became lovers, you didn't trust me enough to tell me the truth." She shook her head. "Whatever we had, whatever I felt for you, has ended."

He flinched as though she had struck him. "Ariel, please. I wanted to tell you, I tried to tell you. But I was so afraid of losing you."

"You don't have to be afraid anymore," she said in a cold voice. "You've already lost me."

The town of San Renaldo had been devastated by the storm. Roofs had been blown off houses. Small huts, much like the ones in the Chontal village, had been flattened. Palm fronds, broken glass and other debris littered the streets and sidewalks.

The tide had risen during the storm, and driven by twenty-foot waves, it had knocked down the pier in the back of the hotel and flooded part of the first floor. The kitchen and the dining room were closed, but the people who had taken refuge in the hotel during the storm were safe.

Ariel's main concern now was for Emory. While Matt and some of the other guests helped *Señor* Lopez clean up, she found a taxi and went to the hospital.

The halls and part of the lobby were crowded with cots. Nurses and doctors hurried among those who had been injured in the storm, and it took a few minutes before Ariel could find out which room Emory was in.

A doctor came out just as she approached, and she said, "I'm Mr. Winston's daughter, doctor. How is he?"

"Much better today, *señorita*." The doctor, obviously anxious to get to all of the other patients, ran an impatient hand through his salt-and-pepper hair. "*Señor* Winston slept all through the storm, and this morning he is free of pain."

"Then it wasn't a heart attack?"

The doctor shook his head. "But it was a strong warning. He obviously has been under a great deal of stress, and he must do something to alleviate that or he will suffer damage to his heart. I have given him medicine to help him relax, and I want him to continue it until he leaves here. When he returns to the United States he should see his doctor immediately."

"When will he be able to leave the hospital?"

"In three or four days." A nurse signaled to him, and he said, "I'm sorry, *señorita*, but there are many that need my attention this morning. You must excuse me now."

Ariel nodded, and when he turned away she opened the door and went into Emory's room. He lay on his side, his eyes closed, his breathing regular. There were dark circles under his eyes, and he was still pale, but he looked better than he had the day before.

She said his name softly, and when he didn't awaken she took the straight-backed chair that was in one corner of the room and pulled it close to the bed. Almost an hour passed before he opened his eyes. "Ariel," he said then. "Dear girl. How long have you been here?"

"Not too long." She took his hand. "How are you feeling?"

"Sleepy. Relaxed as a seal with a full stomach." He yawned and sat up. "What happened to the hurricane? Did it bypass Mexico?"

Ariel laughed and shook her head. "It hit us head-on last night. But you slept through it."

"You're kidding. Really? What happened? Are you all right? What about Matt?"

"We're both fine. The window in our...in the room blew out, and everything's a mess, though. Part of the downstairs of the hotel is flooded, but *Señor* Lopez, the man who drove us here, is cleaning it out. Matt's helping him." She smoothed the hair back from Emory's forehead. "Are you sure you're feeling all right?"

"I'm just a little tired, that's all. It wasn't a heart attack, you know."

"I know."

"So there's no reason why I can't check out of here right now."

"Yes, there is. The doctor wants you to stay for a couple of days to rest up."

"But we've got to get back to L.A."

"We will, Emory, but not until you're feeling better."

"I'm better now." He looked at her, then with a sigh leaned back against the pillow and closed his eyes. "I'm sorry about this," he murmured. "But I suppose the doctor's right. I am tired." He opened his eyes and looked at her. "I feel like I've been running for a very long time, Ariel. I'll be so glad when this is all over."

"So will I."

When this is over. When the pain is gone. She thought of the night and of the passion she and Matt had shared.

But passion, as she'd told him this morning, wasn't enough to base a lifetime relationship on. There had to be more, so much more than that.

She would be glad to get back to Los Angeles. When everything had been straightened out, when Emory was safe, she would get on with her life. Her life without Matt.

When Ariel returned to the hotel that afternoon, *Señor* Lopez and his employees were still working. "The *señor* went to find a *larga distancia*, a long distance booth," *Señor* Lopez told Ariel. "I'm afraid all of the telephone lines are down, but he felt it was necessary to try." He took a handkerchief out of his pocket and mopped his forehead. "How is *Señor* Winston?"

"He's doing very well, thank you. But I'm afraid he won't be out of the hospital for several days."

"Then you will stay here, yes?"

Ariel hesitated. Certainly she and Matt needed a place to stay, but the idea of sharing a room with him, and the fear of what might happen if she did, frightened her. Last night mustn't happen again. It—

"Many people checked out this morning," *Señor* Lopez said. "So we have more vacant rooms. *Señor* McKay told me you would prefer a room of your own, so I have arranged for it. And we are repairing the window in the other room."

So Matt had known that she wouldn't want to stay with him. Ariel breathed a sigh of relief. And wondered, at the same time, why she felt so sad.

Anselmo Sortello, the chief of police of San Renaldo, was a dark-skinned man in his middle fifties. He looked at the credentials on the desk in front of him: Matt's

California driver's license, his business card that said he was a vice president of Continental Trust, and a letter from Lieutenant Martin Brezinski of the Los Angeles Police Department.

"Bueno, señor," Sortello said. "You seem to be who you say you are. Now I need to know more about these men that are looking for you."

"I don't know very much, only that the tall, thin man I told you about is named Ramon. He called the other man Victor. They were both of Mexican descent, but their accents were American. I have no idea who the other men they've hired are."

"I'm aware of the Colombian drug cartel, of course." Sortello leaned back in his chair. "What the United States does not realize is that this is as much our problem as it is theirs and that we too fight every day to put an end to it." He opened a box of cigars on his desk and offered one to Matt. "These are Havanas," he said. "Not as good as in the old days, but still better than any others."

"Thanks," Matt said, and reached for one.

After they had lighted up, Sortello said, "As soon as the telephone lines are working, I will contact the federal police and give them the descriptions you have given me of the two men who are looking for you. When do you expect to leave San Renaldo?"

"I wouldn't think before three or four days," Matt said. "As I told you, Miss Winston's stepfather is in the hospital. As soon as he's feeling better, I'll rent a car."

"You may not be able to do that here, *Señor* McKay, but I can have one of my men drive you into Veracruz, and you will be able to rent one there for the trip to Mexico City. Check with the *federales* before you leave Veracruz. They want to catch these criminals just as much as you do. They'll arrange to have roadblocks set up."

Matt stood and offered his hand. "Thank you, Chief Sortello, I appreciate your help." He tapped the ashes off the end of the cigar. "And I appreciate the cigar."

It was almost dark by the time Matt got back to the hotel. He felt awkward about seeing Ariel. Although her words had cut deep this morning, he understood what she was going through. He would have to wait until all of this was behind them, and they were safely back in Los Angeles. Maybe then she would listen to him, maybe then he could make her understand that though his original plan had been to use her to get to her stepfather, he'd fallen in love with her very early on. Somehow, some way, he had to convince her of his love. He simply could not conceive of living his life without her.

Señor Lopez told Matt which room Ariel had taken, and Matt went upstairs and knocked on the door. "I need to talk to you," he said when she appeared. And before she could answer, he said, "About our plans when we leave."

"All right," she said, and stepped back for him to enter.

"How's Emory?" he asked once he was inside.

"Much better. The doctor has given him medicine to help him to relax, and he sleeps most of the time."

"When do you think he'll get out of the hospital?"

"In a day or two."

"That's good news. He's a nice man, I like him."

"And that surprises you?"

"Yes, it does." She hadn't asked him to sit down, and he stood awkwardly by the door. "I went to see the chief of police this afternoon," he said. "As soon as the phone lines open up, he's going to get in touch with the *feder-ales*. They'll be on the lookout for the two men who've been after us. When Winston's okay, Sortello will have one of his men drive us in to Veracruz. We'll rent a car there and go on to Mexico City.''

"I see."

"I thought I'd go on over to the hospital and see Emory tonight. Are you going?''

Ariel shook her head. "The doctor said it would be better if I didn't disturb him. I'll see him in the morning.''

"Have you had dinner?''

"Yes, I ate when I came back from the hospital.''

"Was it enough? Wouldn't you like something else?''

"No, thank you," she said politely, coolly. "I'll have some fruit later if I'm hungry.''

"Well, then . . ." Matt opened the door. There was so much more he wanted to say, so much more he wanted to do. But he knew he couldn't, not now.

When Ariel closed the door behind him, he stood there, looking at it. Then with a sigh he went down the corridor to his own room.

The three of them left San Renaldo at the end of the week. Emory, looking better and younger than he'd looked when Matt first met him, was in good spirits. He sat up front with Chief Sortello's deputy and chatted all the way to Veracruz.

They checked into the Hotel Emporio there and took rooms facing the harbor and the *malecón*. As before, Matt and Emory shared a room. And Ariel was grateful that they did, for although the doctor in San Renaldo had told her that Emory's condition wasn't serious, she didn't like the idea of his being alone at night.

As for Matt, he had grown increasingly fond of Ariel's stepfather. As they talked and became friends, he began to understand how Emory had been innocently drawn into the money-laundering scheme of the Colombian drug cartel.

Matt got in touch with the *federales*, and he and Emory spent one afternoon looking at mug shots. Neither one of them had gotten a really close look at the men. Matt had seen the man called Ramon at the airport in Acapulco, and seen the two of them through the shadows of his hiding place in the jungle. Emory had only a glimpse of them when they'd assaulted the house. They both agreed on the photo of the tall, skinny man. His name was Ramon Ortega.

One of the *federales* whistled. "Ramon is quite a boy," he said. "He's the suspected head of one of the Culiacan families. He's a murderer, and he's wanted in every state from the Texas border all the way down to the Yucatán." He shook his head. "If he's running things, you can be sure he'll hire all the hoods he needs to track you down. The sooner you're out of Mexico, the better it will be."

"We're leaving for Veracruz tomorrow," Matt told him.

"Okay." The *federale* studied the map. "We'll have roadblocks near Córdoba, Orizaba and Acatzingo. If he's on the road, we'll get him. If we had more men I'd give a police escort, but I'm afraid that's impossible. As soon as you get to Mexico City check in with our office there. A couple of their men will stick with you until you're on the plane for Los Angeles."

Matt stood up and held his hand out. "We're grateful for your help," he said.

"What time are you leaving tomorrow?"

"Early."

"Very good. It's less than three hundred miles from here to Mexico City, but there are mountains and many twists and turns in the road. Go carefully and keep your eye on your rearview mirror. It would embarrass me if your car went out of control and wound up three or four thousand feet down the side of a mountain."

"That's a cheerful thought," Emory said when they left the federal building.

"Yeah, isn't it?" Matt took a deep breath and knew he'd be glad when this was over and they were safely back in the States. He glanced at Emory. "How're you feeling?" he asked.

"Good. I got enough rest in the hospital to last me a lifetime." They headed toward the malecón, and when they reached it, Emory said, "How're things with you and Ariel?"

"The same."

"I'm sorry, Matt. I thought maybe while I was in the hospital the two of you might get together and patch things up. I rather hoped you would."

"Thanks, Emory. But no, we didn't patch things up." Matt shrugged, then said, "Maybe someday."

But in his heart he feared that someday would never come.

They were on the road at seven. Emory, at Ariel's insistence, sat in the front of the gray Volkswagen with Matt. The day before, they had all gone shopping, and now she wore a simple blue dress and high-heeled white shoes. Other things, as well as clothes for Emory and Matt, were packed in a suitcase in the trunk.

They stopped at the first roadblock half an hour out of Veracruz and were waved on after only a cursory glance inside the car. Matt looked in the rearview mirror and saw that the cars after him were waved through just as easily. He didn't like that.

They stopped in Córdoba for breakfast. From there to Orizaba they would be in rough, mountainous country. If anybody was following them, this is where they would strike.

There were few cars on the road. For the first time in his life, Matt wished there was more traffic.

The weather had been clear when they left Veracruz, but here, high up in the mountains, there were low clouds and fog. He had to slow down and turn his headlights on because it was difficult to see the highway curves through the mist.

Emory turned in his seat. "Are you comfortable, honey?" he asked Ariel. "Would you like to change..." He stopped. "There's a car behind us," he told Matt. "Driver doesn't have any lights."

"Maybe he doesn't have any." Matt speeded up. "Let's see if we can lose him. Keep your eye on him, Emory."

Matt tightened his hands around the wheel. He speeded up. They approached a curve. He took it fast, then leveled out.

"He's right behind us," Emory reported.

Matt swore under his breath. He looked in the rearview mirror. The car behind was gaining on them, and now its lights were on, too brightly, almost blinding Matt in the glare when he checked the side-view mirror.

A shot rang out. "Get down!" he cried.

A bullet pinged against the back fender.

The road flattened out in front of them. Matt speeded up again. The little Volkswagen shot forward, but the other car was right behind them.

"They're gaining on us, Matt," Ariel said.

Matt shoved his foot down hard on the gas pedal. Not wanting to take his eyes off the road ahead, he said, "What's happening?"

"They're still gaining on us."

Ahead of him, through the mist, he saw a corkscrew sign and the words *Curva Peligrosa*, dangerous curve. He had to slow down; he didn't have any choice.

"Take the gun out of my waistband," he told Emory as he started into the curve. "If you can get a clear shot, try for one of the tires or the windshield."

"Right." Emory rolled his window down. "All right," he murmured. "They're coming around the curve. Hold her steady." He turned around and, leaning out the window, fired, then swore.

There was an answering shot. Matt yanked Emory back inside. More shots rang out. The car swerved. "Tire," Emory yelled.

Matt fought to control the car. It swerved toward the edge of the mountain. He hauled back on the steering wheel. Through the mist he saw a clump of bushes and headed for it.

"Jump out when I stop," he cried. "Head for the bushes." He grabbed the gun from Emory, braked, swung the car sideways, then shouted. "Now! Get out! I'll cover you."

Emory half fell out of the front, regained his footing, then reached in the back for Ariel and pulled her after him. The car behind them slowed, skidded on the wet road, then screeched to a stop.

Matt scrambled out of the Volkswagen. Using the car as a shield, he fired off a round of shots.

Two men jumped out of the car, shooting as they came. Matt darted a look to the side. Ariel and Emory were almost to the bushes.

Another man jumped out of the car. Firing, he ran toward them. Matt raised his gun and fired. The man spun around and dropped. The other two men advanced, one toward the side of the road where Ariel and Emory had sought shelter. The other man, the tall skinny guy Matt had first seen at the airport in Acapulco, came toward him.

Ariel and Emory were unarmed. Matt had to stop the man going toward them, but in order to do it he had to leave the shelter of the car. He saw the other man's arm rise, and he ran from the shelter, shooting as he ran. The man clutched his chest and fell backward without a sound.

Matt, out in the open now, sprinted for the bushes. Suddenly he fell. Hell of a time to stumble, he thought. Then he felt the hot, burning pain and knew he'd been shot.

He lay on his back, stunned, unable for a moment to move. He heard Ariel scream, and when he looked up he saw her running toward him.

"No!" he cried. "Get back!"

The tall, skinny man pointed his gun at her. And Matt, with the last ounce of his strength, raised his gun and fired. His enemy spun around. There was a look of surprise on his cadaverous face. Then, like an accordion, his tall, thin body folded and fell.

Everything got blurry. It's the mist, Matt thought. It's blinding me. I can't see. I can't . . .

He heard Ariel's voice calling to him. He tried to tell her that everything was all right, that he was tired, that he'd only rest a little while. He felt her take his hand. From a far distance he heard her calling to him. Then the mist became blackness, and the blackness covered him.

When Matt awoke, he was flat on his back, going down a long corridor. Ariel was beside him, holding his hand.

"Where'm I?" he whispered in a voice that didn't sound like his."

"You're in a hospital in Orizaba," she said.

"I got shot. Is it my leg? Is it bad?"

"No. But they're . . . they're taking you into surgery, Matt. They—"

"I'm sorry, *señorita*," a strange voice said. "You must leave him now."

He felt the pressure of her hand on his before she let him go. They wheeled him into a brightly lit room. He knew he'd lost her again.

"Don't . . ." He tried to form the words. "Don't go away," he whispered.

"I won't," he thought he heard her say just before someone jabbed a needle into his arm and a doctor with a white mask half covering his face said, "Say *buenos noches, señor*."

Chapter 17

Five days after the surgery, the doctor who had operated on Matt in Orizaba had him sent by ambulance to Mexico City. Emory rode up front with the driver, Ariel rode in the back with Matt.

In pain, and weak from loss of blood, Matt drifted in and out of consciousness. And in that state of semiconsciousness he dreamed that he and Ariel were back in Zipolite, swimming in a sea turned golden in the sun. The waves brought her salt-slick body against his, and he kissed her. She said, "No, no, no. Never again, Matthew," and disappeared under a wave.

"Wait!" he cried, and began to swim after her, down deep under the sea, straining to see through the cloudy dimness of musky water. At last he saw her, lithe and pale and lovely, her long hair, like silver seaweed, floating with the current. She looked over her shoulder and slowly shook her head, then turned and began to swim away from him.

"Wait!" he cried, panicked, afraid. "Don't leave me. I can't breathe down here. I can't..."

"Shh," Ariel said, "I'm here. We're taking you to Mexico City. Hang on, Matt. Just hang on."

He closed his eyes before he saw the tears streaming down her cheeks.

For as long as she lived, Ariel would never forget that terrible moment when Matt fell wounded and bleeding. She'd run to him, screaming, trying to staunch the blood while Emory flagged down a car.

She hadn't left his side, except when they operated on his leg in Orizaba, and she was with him now, on her knees, holding him when the ambulance jarred over a rough portion of the road or sped around the curve of a mountain.

"*Señor* McKay's leg is very bad," the doctor who did the surgery had said. "There's a great deal of muscle damage, and in my opinion more surgery will be necessary before it is completely well. Even then I'm not sure the leg will be as it once was. The bullet did a lot of damage, but the specialist I'm sending you to in Mexico City is a good man. Perhaps he will be able to do more for *Señor* McKay than I am able to do."

Ariel spent that first night in Mexico City at Matt's bedside, and she was with him the next morning when the doctor examined him.

"I concur with my colleague in Orizaba," he told Matt. "You do need additional surgery. I would like to schedule it as soon as you're feeling a little better."

"Will that do it?" Matt asked. "Will my leg be okay then?"

"It will take a few weeks before we know for sure, *Señor* McKay. If it isn't, then an additional operation will be necessary. I would prefer, because of the difficulty of the trip, that you stay here until you have fully recovered. But if you choose to return to California, I will do my best to make you as comfortable as I can."

Matt looked at Ariel. "What do you think I should do?"

She took a deep shaking breath. "It . . . it's your decision, Matt."

He turned back to the doctor. "I'll have the surgery here," he said. A muscle jumped in his cheek. "There's no reason for me to go back to California right now." He looked at her. "Is there?"

Lower lip caught between her teeth, she shook her head and said, "No, there isn't."

The next night, when Emory came to see him, Matt said, "I talked to Lieutenant Brezinski. He'll have two of his men meet you and Ariel at the plane in L.A. From there you'll be taken to my home in Santa Barbara."

"I wish you were going with us, Matt."

"I wouldn't be much help with this leg, Emory, and it doesn't seem to make much difference whether I'm stuck in the hospital here or in L.A. Right now, I guess I'd rather be here." Matt shifted in the bed. "Once you turn over the money in the Swiss account to Continental Trust, they'll drop the charges. As far as Brezinski is concerned, he's willing to go along with the bank's decision on the condition that you testify when Trevino and his men are rounded up. I told him you would."

"It will give me a great deal of pleasure to do just that."

"Have you got the diamonds?"

"I got them out of the bank this morning."

Matt nodded. "I'll make arrangements for one of the *federales* to be sure you're safely on the plane. When are you leaving?"

"Tomorrow."

"I see." Under cover of the sheet, Matt clenched his hands. "Then what, Emory?" he asked, trying to keep the emotion out of his voice.

"I'm going to finish *Winter Love*. I've talked to a couple of colleagues, old movie buddies. They're willing to put up the money to finish the film in return for a percentage of the profits."

"And after that?"

"I've got a piece of land in Baja, right on the sea of Cortez. I'm going to build a small house there, with a studio where I can paint. Ariel can live there with me if that's what she wants." Emory hesitated. "I wish things were different, Matt."

"Yes, so do I." Matt held his hand out. "You're everything she said you were, Emory. It's been a pleasure getting to know you."

"You too, Matt. When you're better, come on down to Baja. You can help me build the house."

"I might just do that."

"Ariel's waiting outside. She wants to say goodbye."

Matt braced himself. "Okay," he said. "Send her in."

She came in wearing a dark green suit and a white blouse with little ruffles around her throat. She looked fashionable, yet strangely fragile. And tense.

"Well," she said, and cleared her throat. "You're... you're looking much better."

"Yeah, I'm all right."

"Does your leg hurt?"

"Not as much as it did."

"We're leaving tomorrow." She hesitated. "I wouldn't leave, not this soon, but I'll have to testify, along with Emory."

"I know."

"What are you going to do? When the leg is better, I mean."

"I'm not sure. The doctor thinks it'll be two or three months before I'm back on my feet."

"I'm sorry. You were trying to protect us and now you're in pain and I . . ." She shook her head, unable for a moment, to go on. "There's so much I want to say, Matt, but so little I *can* say. I'm sorry about the way things turned out."

"Yes, so am I. Maybe when this is all over, we can—"

She held up her hand. "No," she said. "We can't." She tightened her hands around her purse. "I have to go now. We're leaving in the morning."

"I know." He wanted to touch her. And knew that he couldn't. "Goodbye, Ariel," he said.

"Goodbye, Matt. I . . ."

She hesitated, and a flare of hope kindled deep inside him. He said, "Ariel," and reached out his hand to her.

She shook her head. "No," she whispered, and before he could speak again she turned and ran out the door.

When the trial ended and Trevino and the men of the Colombian connection had been sentenced, Emory gathered his original crew together and began work on *Winter Love.*

A week before it began he had called Steve Mancini and met the actor for lunch. "You weren't my choice to play the role of Philip,'' he told the actor. "I wanted to keep Ken Cameron. But I've looked at what we shot, the earlier version with Cameron and the later version with you playing Philip. You're better than he is. I want you to finish the film.''

"I'm not sure I'm available." Mancini's million-dollar-mouth curled in a supercilious sneer.

"I talked to your agent this morning. You're available." Emory leaned across the table. "*Winter Love* is your shot at the Oscar, Mancini. Don't be a damn fool.''

He'd watched a mixture of emotions play across the actor's handsome face. Then Mancini had said, "I'd damn well better have a decent dressing room this time.''

Ariel found a two-bedroom apartment for herself and Emory in the Hollywood Hills. As soon as the picture was finished, he would move to Baja and start building his house. She didn't know what she would do.

She tried not to think about Matt in the hospital in Mexico City. She knew that Emory spoke to him often and that he would have told her if Matt's recovery hadn't been satisfactory.

The days passed. Ariel went to work with Emory every morning and tried to lose herself in the film. But the nights were bad, and so were the weekends, when her thoughts were filled with Matt and the way it had been in the beginning.

Emory finished *Winter Love* the second week in December and flew down to Baja to begin work on his house there. He tried to get Ariel to go with him, but she demurred.

"I've got a lot to do here," she said.

"But you look tired. We've both been working hard these last few months. You need a change.''

"I just don't feel up to it, Emory. I'd really rather stay here. I promise that I'll sleep late, drink my milk and go to bed early every night."

The apartment seemed empty without him. In spite of her promise to go to bed early, Ariel found that she couldn't sleep. She read, she watched television, she drank warm milk. Nothing helped. It was often three or four in the morning before she finally fell into an exhausted, dream-troubled sleep.

She often thought of Matt. Where was he now? she wondered. Had he come back to L.A. or was he still in Mexico?

A few days before Emory's return she made herself go out and buy a small Christmas tree. She decorated it that night while she watched a rerun of *Cheers* instead of listening to Christmas carols on the radio. "Deck the Halls with Boughs of Holly" would have finished her off.

She was having breakfast the next morning when the package came.

"Sign here," the UPS man said.

There wasn't any name of sender, just the words, "Zipolite, Mexico."

With trembling fingers, Ariel unwrapped the package and saw the music box.

She lifted it out and held it close to her for a moment before she took off the top and listened to the soft, tinny music of "As Time Goes By."

"You must remember this . . ."

"Matt," she wept. "Oh, Matt."

He was swimming hard, taking pleasure in the smooth feel of the water on his almost naked body and of the sun on his face. Every day his leg grew stronger and he walked with only a barely discernible limp.

He knew it was time to go back, but still he waited. Waited and hoped.

Matt rolled onto his back, and gazing up at the blue sky, he conjured figures out of the clouds the way he'd done when he was a child. And tried not to think of Ariel.

Had she received the music box yet? He tried to picture her opening it. He hoped it hadn't made her unhappy. That wasn't what he wanted.

He swam toward shore, and when he came up onto the beach he sluiced the water off his lean, tanned body, slung a towel over his shoulders, and started back to the cabana.

He'd been right to come here to heal. This was the place where he had fallen in love with Ariel. There were memories of her here by the sea; he felt closer to her here.

But there was pain in remembrance. He turned and looked back at the water. He thought of that early morning when they'd run naked into the waves, and how afterward they had made love in the same cabana he had now. In the soft rush of the waves he heard again her sighs and her whispers, her sweet cries of passion.

He dug his toes into the hot sand, reluctant to leave the sun for the shaded solitude of the place he had once shared with Ariel.

Suddenly Matt stopped, listening, because it seemed to him that he could hear the faint, tinkling sounds of the music box. He ran his hands across his eyes. He'd been so deep in his thoughts of her that now he was hearing things. He . . .

Then, with a low cry, he ran forward, her name on his lips, scarcely believing, praying... He paused in the open doorway, and he saw her, standing only a few feet away.

For a moment she didn't speak. Then she said, "Matt? I've come back, Matt. If you still want me—"

"Want you?" His voice choked with emotion. He took her in his arms. "Ariel," he said against the sweet cloud of her hair. "Oh, Ariel."

Then he kissed her. And all that had passed before faded in the glory of the kiss and the promise of all that was to come.

* * * * *

✦ *Silhouette Intimate Moments* ®

COMING NEXT MONTH

#333 CORRUPTED—Beverly Sommers

Police officer Sandy McGee is on special assignment to protect Johnny Random, a crooked cop. In a world of false identities and misplaced trust, in which even the double-crossers are double-crossed, Sandy, torn between her ethics and her growing passion for Johnny, must choose: honor or love? Or can she have both?

#334 SOMEONE TO TURN TO— Marilyn Cunningham

Ramsey Delacroix returns to her grandfather's ranch after a shattering divorce. Instead of the safety and reassurance she craves, she finds murder. Compelled to defend her family, yet helpless against her deepening feelings for the bitter Brad Chillicott, Ramsey is forced to choose between loyalty to her family and a dangerous love for a stranger.

#335 LOVING LIES—Ann Williams

To catch a killer, Lauren Downing finds herself recruited as bait. Working alongside the town's "bad boy," Jesse Tyler, in a race against time, she discovers a deepening passion that goes against all the rules. Despite the odds, they must reveal the killer's identity—will it be in time to save their growing love?

#336 DREAM CHASERS— Mary Anne Wilson

TV host Jillian Segar, on assignment in volatile South America with her enigmatic former lover Carson Davies, finds herself enmeshed in a web of political intrigue. Irresistibly drawn to Carson, and finding herself falling in love, Jillian must put her life in his hands. Can he be trusted to save her, or will love elude them once again?

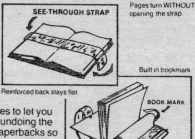

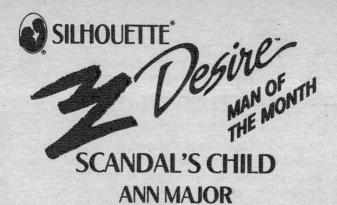